Pilgrims and Time Travelers

Collected Short Stories:
Volume 1

JOE VASICEK

Other books by Joe Vasicek

Genesis Earth Trilogy
Genesis Earth
Edenfall
The Stars of Redemption

Gunslinger Trilogy
Gunslinger to the Stars
Gunslinger to the Galaxy
Gunslinger to Earth

Gaia Nova
Bringing Stella Home
Desert Stars
Stars of Blood and Glory
Heart of the Nebula

Sons of the Starfarers
Brothers in Exile
Comdrades in Hope
Strangers in Flight
Friends in Command
Patriots in Retreat
A Queen in Hiding
An Empire in Disarray
Victors in Liberty

Pilgrims and Time Travelers

Collected Short Stories: Volume 1

JOE VASICEK

CONTENTS

The Gettysburg Paradox

"Fix bayonets!"

The order from Colonel Lawrence Chamberlain filled Leroy with a thrill unlike any he'd ever known. This was it—the moment he'd waited so long for. The moment he'd traveled almost two hundred years through history to experience.

All around him, the dead and dying bodies of men in blue and gray littered the forested slopes of Little Round Top. The biting stench of musket smoke hung like brimstone in the air, while the thunder of enemy cannon boomed in the distance like the drums of hell. Leroy's hands shook as he clumsily fitted the bayonet to the end of his rifle. He had known that the fighting would be hard, but nothing could have prepared him for this. Wave after wave of Confederate soldiers had charged endlessly up the hill, reaping death and carnage. A part of him screamed to use the timeslip device in his coat pocket to escape the horrors of the battlefield, but he grit his teeth and forced the cowardly thought from his mind.

This is it, he told himself, *the greatest moment of glory you will ever know.* The charge of the Twentieth Maine—the daring bayonet charge that had single-handedly saved the Union Army on the second day of the Battle of Gettysburg. In that moment, when the outcome of the battle—indeed, of the war itself—stood poised on the edge of a knife, those three hundred Mainers had done more to affect the course of history than any other regiment in the war. And now, Leroy was about to be a part of it.

"Right wheel forward!" came Chamberlain's piercing voice, and the blast of the bugle sounded like the trumpets of a heavenly host. Now the left flank took up the yell, sweeping down to meet the rebels head-on. The sharpshooters of Company B, hidden behind a stone wall down the slope to the east, stood and fired into the Confederate flank, sowing death and confusion among their ranks.

Now Leroy's company had taken up the charge, and he was running headlong down the hill with the rest of them. The battle cries of the men in blue stirred something primal in his heart, and the horrors of the battlefield blurred before him. All he knew was smoke and sweat and dust and blood.

All around him, the men of the Fifteenth Alabama dropped their muskets and lifted their hands in surrender. Others tried to run, tripping over the rough terrain or falling to the ground in exhaustion. The charge gave way to a route as the men of the Twentieth Maine reduced the rebels to a disorganized mob.

Leroy ran breathlessly with his musket held high. About halfway down the hill, he stopped in front of a gray-coated rebel who had risen unsteadily to his feet. The man raised his hands in surrender, but his eyes were full of fury, not fear.

That was when Leroy saw the timeslip device gripped firmly in his right hand.

"The South will rise again!" he shouted before disappearing into thin air. Stunned, it was all Leroy could do to hold onto his musket.

"What the..." His breath came in short gasps, but his mind raced in horror. Time travelers in the Fifteenth Alabama? But the Temporal Police strictly forbade time tourists from taking a side that could change the course of history. Indeed, Leroy had only managed to join the Twentieth Maine by hiring a black market Russian company to insert him. But if there were time tourists on both sides...

The union soldiers streamed all around him as the charge continued down the hill, but Leroy hardly noticed them. The fury in the rebel time traveler's eyes still haunted him, and his parting words—"the South will rise again!"—rang like the thunder of cannon fire in his ears.

Night fell soon after the main assault, but skirmishing continued long into the evening. Leroy gripped his musket with sweaty hands as the crack of potshots sounded down the hill. With the other soldiers of the Twentieth Maine, he spent most of the evening moving rebel prisoners. By the time he had returned to the camp, the twilight was fading and the stars were shining in the nineteenth century night.

Far from reveling in the historic victory that had been his privilege to witness, Leroy couldn't stop thinking about the time traveling Confederate soldier. He knew fully well the significance of the events he had just experienced. The Civil War had been a lifetime obsession with him, and he'd spent more than ten million twenty-second century dollars for the privilege of witnessing the war's most crucial turning point firsthand. But now, doubts were beginning to creep up on him—doubts about the effectiveness of the Temporal Police, and the historical purity of the battle.

When a time tourist went back to some great and pivotal event, there was always a danger that the flow of the timeline would be altered. Normally, events had a way of working themselves out, and when tourists were too careless, the Temporal Police would swoop in and arrest them before their carelessness led to disaster. Thus, continuity of the timeline was strictly preserved.

But how could the Temporal Police have allowed anyone to fight on the Confederate side? The fighting on Little Round Top had been so tenuous, something as small as a stray bullet could have changed everything. If Colonel Chamberlain had been killed before ordering his boys to fix bayonets, or if Lieutenant Melcher had been shot down as he ran at the head of the charge, the day could have ended in disaster. Why then had there been time travelers on both sides of the engagement? Had a tourist somehow slipped past the watchful eyes of the Temporal Police? Or worse, had some insane fanatic gained access to a timeslip device?

Leroy had no answers to these disturbing questions. He considered using the timeslip device to return to the twenty-second century and inform the authorities, but that would mean giving up his chance to witness Pickett's Charge on the third day. With the strings he'd had to pull and the hoops he'd had to jump through just to join the Twentieth Maine, he doubted that he'd get another chance to come back to Gettysburg once he'd left.

There was another option, though. On the long march to Gettysburg, Leroy had noticed a soldier in Company B fiddling with what had looked like a timeslip device. Important historical events like Gettysburg always brought in a hefty profit, so it made sense that Leroy wasn't the only time traveler. Neither of them had spoken to each other—for all Leroy knew, the man still thought of himself as the only time tourist in the regiment—but if there was anyone Leroy could speak to about his concerns, it was him.

He found the sharpshooters of Company B gathered around a campfire, laughing and smiling as they exchanged stories. A couple tin flasks of spirits were making their way around, and the rosy cheeks and bloodshot eyes showed that the festivities had been going on for some time.

The time tourist was right in the thick of them, laughing as hard as any of the others. Leroy hesitated, wondering if now was a good time. He stepped back into woods and pulled out his timeslip device, setting it back an hour from the present.

After a brief moment of disorientation, he looked up to find the sky still lit in the purple hues of twilight. A short distance away, the men of Company B had just sat down to supper, with tin plates in their laps and a steaming pot of porridge suspended over the fire. The men carried on just as merrily as before, but were much more sober. The time tourist was seated on the exact same rock as before—or as after.

Leroy took a deep breath and stepped out of the shadowy wood.

"Good evening, gentlemen."

"Evening, Corporal," said the senior sergeant. "What can we do for you?"

"I would like to have a word, if I may, with private..." Leroy stared at the time tourist, his name suddenly escaping him.

"Private Jones?"

"Yes, Private Jones. It's about a personal matter."

Private Jones rose slowly to his feet, a queer look on his face. "Corporal Leroy, is it? What can I do for you?"

Leroy took the man by the arm and led him away from his comrades, who stared flatly at them as they left. "There's something we need to talk about where the others can't hear us."

"What do you mean?"

Leroy fished into his coat and pulled out the timeslip device. "I trust that you recognize—"

"Oh, another time traveler!" said Jones, loud enough that everyone could hear him. "Come, why don't you join us?"

Leroy's eyes widened as Private Jones pulled him back to the campfire. The men of Company B rose and greeted him with brotherly slaps and vigorous handshakes. Far from shock and disbelief at the discovery of a time traveler in their midst, the men greeted him as if he were one of their own.

"Another one, eh? Which company are you attached with?"

"Are you twenty-second century or twenty-third?"

"Lovely battle today, wasn't it? Lovely!"

"But—but" Leroy stammered. His stomach grew sick as realization slowly dawned on him. The men around the campfire—indeed, almost the whole of Company B—weren't nineteenth-century natives at all, but time travelers just like him.

"Have a seat, have a seat," said the senior sergeant, a round-faced Irish man with fiery eyes and a thick red beard. "Corporal Leroy, is it? Sergeant Owens of the twenty-second century, pleased to be making your acquaintance, sir!"

"You're all time travelers?"

Owens chuckled and slapped him heartily on the back. "That we are, lad, that we are. Oh, not the whole company—Captain Morrill is native—but as for the rest of us, let's just say that we've come a long way to see this day."

"But you were the ones who fired into the rebel flank during the bayonet charge," said Leroy, his heart racing. "If it weren't for your company, the rebel line might have held, and—"

"—and the brave charge of the Twentieth Maine would have ended in disaster," Owens interjected. "A good thing we showed up in time then, eh boys?"

The men roared with laughter at the offhanded joke. Leroy only stared at them dumbfounded, his eyes wide with horror.

"You deliberately altered the timeline?"

"Bloody right we did," said Owens, the Irish twang in his voice ringing like a bell. "And a right good thing too."

"But what about the Temporal Police? Didn't they try to stop you?"

"You mean Hitler's time cronies?" one of the men asked.

"We took care of them when we joined the Twentieth Maine," Jones explained. "Gave them a proper run-around."

"Only some of them, though," said Owens, his eyes gleaming. "The rest..." he made a cutting motion across his throat and grinned.

Dear God, Leroy thought. *They killed the Time Police.*

Sergeant Owens pulled out a tin flask of spirits from his coat pocket. "When the Union wins this battle, those rebel dogs will melt away like dew before the sun. Not even Lee's genius will be enough to save them!"

"And the Allies will be a force to be reckoned with!"

"The Third Reich will fall!"

"Wait—the Third Reich?" Leroy asked, his head reeling in confusion. "What are you talking about?"

"Why, the Nazis of course! That's why we're here—to unite the Americans so that they can help us defeat Hitler."

"Oh, I don't know about all that," said a man with a thick black beard. "Hitler's not that bad. I'm just here to prevent the Second Civil War. I want to see this country rise to greatness and take her rightful place in the world."

"He's from a different timeline," Owens said, as if that explained everything. "But one thing we can agree on is that the Union has bloody well got to be preserved."

"Hear hear!"

"Wait—you're from a timeline where we lost the Battle of Gettysburg?" Leroy asked. He looked from man to man, searching their faces in the dim firelight.

Owens frowned at him. "Do you mean to tell us, lad, that where you're from the North wins?"

All at once, the men were in an uproar, clamoring at Leroy with their eager questions.

"What's the future like?"

"How long does it take us to win the war?"

"Which general does Lincoln pick next?"

"Hell—what happens on the battlefield tomorrow?"

"Stop!" Leroy screamed. "Just—just stop it, all of you!"

"That's right," said Owens. "Can't you see you're crowding him? Give the man some air!"

This can't be happening, Leroy thought, his head swimming in confusion. Company B—the Twentieth Maine. They'd only won today because an army of fanatic Union supporters had gone back in time to change history. The charge at Little Round Top, the bravery of men like Lawrence Chamberlain and Patrick O'Rourke—it all seemed so pointless to him now. That moment before the bayonet charge when the outcome of the war had hung as if from a thread—it had never been that close, because the time travelers would never have allowed it.

Then he remembered the Confederate soldier with the timeslip device. *The South will rise again!*

"Wait! Wait," he said, waving at the others for silence. "There's something important I need to tell you—something that could change everything!"

"What is it, Corporal?"

"Quiet—let him speak!"

"The Alabamans—the Fifteenth and the Forty Seventh. They've got time travelers in those regiments!"

Owens frowned, and the others eyed him warily. "What do you mean, lad?"

"The Confederates have got time travelers in their army just like we do! Hood's division, Longstreet's corps—who knows but what Pickett's got them, too!"

"General Pickett? Isn't he in the Confederate rear guard?"

"I thought he came up too late to be part of the fighting."

Sergeant Owens clasped both hands on Leroy's shoulders. "This is very important, lad," he said, his expression deadly serious. "Of all of us, you're the only one who knows what happens tomorrow. What does Lee plan to do?"

"Pickett's charge," Leroy said, barely aware that the words had left his mouth. "The high water mark of the Confederacy. Lee gives Longstreet Trimble and Pettigrew's divisions, and together with General Pickett they charge the center of the Union lines."

The men sobered up at once.

"A Confederate charge at the center of our lines? That could break us!"

"Do the men in the Second Corps know about this?"

"We should call for reinforcements—God knows the Confederates already have."

"It will be the bloodiest battle ever fought on American soil!"

It was *the bloodiest battle ever fought on American soil,* Leroy thought, blood draining from his cheeks once again. The Battle of Gettysburg, almost fifty-thousand casualties from both sides—and how many of them were time travelers? How many of them had invaded this time from the future, fighting on these hallowed fields of the past? It was too much—too much!

"Let me go!" he yelled, shoving Sergeant Owens to the ground. The men leaped, but he ran past them, fumbling in his coat for the timeslip device. The others immediately began to pursue him, but before they could lay hold of him he set the device forward about sixteen hours and engaged.

* * * * *

Leroy tripped and fell flat on his face, dropping the timeslip device in the rotting leaves. When he groaned and got up, the hot July sun was burning the back of his neck, and the thunder of dueling artillery resounded across the Pennsylvania hills.

The Confederate bombardment before Pickett's Charge, he realized. *The largest artillery barrage of the war.* The ground shook as hundreds of cannon bore down on each other.

It was madness—sheer madness. Soldiers from the future fighting a battle in the past. And did Gettysburg even belong to the nineteenth century anymore? Had it ever? States' rights and the Union, secession and the constitution, slavery and equality, freedom and independence, the clash of American civilizations and the baptism by fire of democracy and the modern world. Never before and perhaps never since would so much of the future hang on so brief a moment in history. And so, here they were, men of the twenty-second and twenty-third centuries disguised as natives of the nineteenth to give their lives for the future they had never had. How much of it was even real anymore? How much of it was meddling from so many broken timelines? And what if the war itself was merely a fabrication to bring about this great and terrible day?

I have to stop it, Leroy decided, rising to his feet as the guns thundered in the distance. *I have to pull back the curtain and expose this charade for what it is.*

He stumbled wildly through the forest, trying to figure out his next move. The artillery barrage would be over within the hour, and the Confederate troops of Longstreet's corps would begin their terrible charge. There would be a moment of calm as they entered the killing field, and then all hell would descend upon the men of both sides. If he was to stop the battle, he had to get to them before that.

He came upon the site of the fighting yesterday, where the fight for Little Round Top had been at its worst. Stillness shrouded the hill today, with bodies in blue and gray littering the ground like rotting leaves. Leroy searched frantically among them until he found a soldier with a shirt that could pass as white. He cut it off the stiffened corpse with a nearby bayonet and fashioned it into something resembling a flag of truce. Then, tying it to the end of a musket, he sprinted back to the union lines.

The guns had stopped, and an unearthly silence descended upon the battlefield. Leroy, short of breath, ran into the camp.

I'll never get out there on foot, he realized. *I'll have to ride out on horseback.*

He found a horse tied next to the Colonel's tent. A couple of swarthy soldiers smoked pipes and played cards on a large, flat rock nearby. Leroy didn't bother to see who they were. He untied the horse and leaped to the saddle.

"What the deuce?"

"Stop him!"

The horse whinnied and rose up on its hind legs as he spurred it to action. One man grasped at the reins, only to be knocked aside while the other drew his pistol. Moments later, Leroy was galloping down the hillside, bullets shrieking inches from his ears as the flag of truce flapped wildly by his side.

He tore past the rocks of Devil's Den and onto the road leading to the Wheat field. Rebel skirmishers fired potshots at him, so he turned off and headed north. Up ahead, at the base of the slopes leading up to Cemetery Ridge, the Virginians of Pickett's division were advancing, their bayonets glistening in the sun. A shout went up from the union ranks, sheltered behind the stone wall at the top. Over the furious pounding of his horse's hooves, Leroy made out the words "Fredericksburg! Fredericksburg!"

"Stop!" he yelled. "Stop!"

On the field ahead of him, thousands of Confederate soldiers marched proudly in their ranks across the wide, deadly space between the armies. It was their greatest moment of glory, the last day of hope for the dream of the Confederacy, and it seemed that all the South had assembled to be there.

"Stop!" Leroy screamed, pulling out onto the Emmitsburg road. He held up the flag of truce and waved it with all his strength.

"We're all time travelers! We're all time travelers! Can't you see? We're all—"

A cannon shell burst in front of him, kicking up great clods of earth and throwing him from his horse. The world around him spun drunkenly and turned dark.

He gasped for breath, tasting dirt and blood. He'd lost all feeling in his legs, but that was nothing to the ringing in his ears. He opened his eyes and saw only blurry, indistinct shapes—the green grass, the blue sky, some gray movement off to his side. Then an explosion sounded nearby him, and his mind suddenly cleared.

The Union artillery was firing at the rebels—firing and taking them out ten at a time. The whistle of cannonballs and the bursting of shells filled his world, and he covered his head in terror.

Now the troops were marching past him, marching in their long proud lines as the artillery all but decimated them. The rebel yell mingled with the other sounds of battle, and the ground shook not only with cannon fire but the tread of thousands of feet.

The timeslip device, Leroy thought weakly. He reached into his coat pocket but it wasn't there. As his vision cleared and the troops marched around him, he saw it in the grass just out of his reach. An explosion made him duck, casting great clods of dirt all over him. Whether out of courage or desperation, he rallied his strength and crawled on his elbows toward his only means of escape.

Just as his hand grasped the timeslip device, a leather-booted foot stomped it down. He looked up at the black-bearded face of a man in gray uniform.

"We're... we're all... we're all—"

"Time travelers?" the man said. "We know."

He grinned and cocked his pistol. A burst of smoke, a jolt of pain, and Leroy's time ceased forever.

Killing Mister Wilson

On my first run with the time machine, I took a watch. On my second, I took a gun.

You see, there was someone in my timeline who was so monstrous and vile, whose crimes against humanity were so horrific, that any time traveler would have had a moral obligation to see him dead. He was so evil, in fact, that in my timeline Godwin's law referred to him instead of Stalin (yes, we had our own version of Godwin's law. Yes, I know it's an ironic coincidence. I'm a time traveler—I'm used to these sorts of things by now).

How evil was he, exactly? Well, let me put it this way. You know the Armenian Holocaust? The Stalinist Gulag? The Imperial Japanese purges of the east? All of these crimes were dwarfed by the evils that were committed in this man's name (yes, even the Gulag—in this timeline, at least). He was also responsible for renewing the Great War and plunging the whole world into it. But that is not all. In this war, atomic power was harnessed to create a superweapon—yes, atomic power. It was exactly as horrific as you imagine. Before we put a man in space, we had the capacity to annihilate our entire species.

So you can see why I had a moral obligation to stop this man. It was so blatantly obvious that even our time travel stories had turned it into a cliché.

Before I left, I researched my target carefully. I spent years studying history to determine the best place to eliminate my target before the course of history was locked. Once that was done, I carefully selected the place and time for the hit, down to the very precise minute and the exact location in which he would be. For the instrument of death, I selected a Browning 50 calibre sniper rifle. You aren't familiar with the weapon since it doesn't exist in your timeline. All you need to know is that it was more than capable of bringing down a target at a large distance.

The event was an open air parade, my vantage point, an abandoned building some two city blocks away. I arrived in the early morning, and set up for the gruesome deed just as the crowds were starting to gather. With the patience of a man who literally has all the time in the world, I waited for the festivities to begin. And when my target came into view of the cheering crowds, standing in the back of his black Pierce-Arrow, I cocked my weapon and steadied my aim.

A sharp crack, a sudden jolt, and President Woodrow Wilson fell dead.

Yes, I was the one who assassinated President Wilson in 1916. No, I wasn't part of some grand conspiracy. I've seen the footage from the parade, and while yes, it clearly shows the shot coming from the opposite direction according to the official reports, the conspiracy theorists make far more of that point than it actually deserves. In any case, long before the investigation knew where to look, I'd erased any trace that I'd ever been there.

Why President Wilson, you ask? Was he the man who committed all those awful crimes? No, not exactly. But you must understand, in order to effectively change history, you have to address the systemic underlying causes, not merely the symptomatic effects. It's a bit like the dragonfly in that story by Ray Bradbury (though in our timeline, it was a butterfly).

You see, in my timeline, the United States did not remain neutral in the Great War. Yes, I know that we supplied arms and supplies to the allies since practically the beginning of the war. But in my timeline, President Wilson sent a million-man army to Europe in 1917, forcing the Germans' hand and tipping the war decisively against them. God knows the wheels were already starting to turn by the time I intervened, but with Wilson out of the picture, those plans were put on hold. And when the 1918 flu pandemic struck the world, our problems back home were so severe that military adventurism was completely out of the picture.

How did the Great War end in my timeline? Decisively. The Allies beat the snot out of the Central Powers and brought the Germans to their knees. Their postwar economy tanked so bad, they were using bank notes to wallpaper their houses. Yes, I know that's hard for you to believe. But in my timeline, it really happened.

You see, the Germans also made the transition from empire to republic in my timeline, but the war had smashed them so badly that the republic promptly collapsed, and a totalitarian nightmare rose in its place. At least in this timeline, the armistice bought them enough time to make the transition properly.

The thirties and forties were a dark time for you, but believe me, they were far, far worse in my timeline. Do I regret killing President Wilson? I only regret that it was necessary. No one is innocent in the eyes of history.

Before you go, there is one last thing I'd like to share with you. Do you see that painting on my wall? No, don't apologize—I'm not offended that you missed it. It looks a bit like a postcard, with the flags of the League of Nations flying in front of the Reichstag. The composition is well-done, but otherwise unremarkable. It was a gift to me from the German ambassador to the league, who painted it himself. As you can see, his signature is in the bottom-right corner: *A. Hitler.*

My Name Is For My Friends

The stranger walked up to Jabeg's campfire, a longsword sheathed at his waist. "Good evening," he said. "Mind if I join you?"

Jabeg's blood ran cold. He glanced sidelong at his sword, which lay propped up against his saddlebags just outside of his reach. He had two throwing knives in his boots, and a dagger on the rock beside him, but none of those were any match for a longsword at close range.

"What do you want?" he asked, his voice low.

"Something to eat," said the stranger, grunting at the question. "What are you cooking?"

Both men eyed each other uneasily. The stranger had a beard that was long for a soldier, but short for a bandit. His eyes were a bright, piercing blue, his hair an auburn blond like the men of the Northland plains. Both of his thumbs were hooked over his belt, but Jabeg didn't doubt that he could draw his sword in a second. The fact that he'd snuck up on the camp unawares made it clear enough that he was not a naive traveler looking only for food.

"Are you on foot?" Jabeg asked. He carefully withdrew his hand and leaned forward, bringing it within reach of his hidden throwing knife.

The stranger's eyes narrowed. "Only a fool would travel this road by foot—and with all the bandits, he wouldn't make it far."

You didn't answer my question, Jabeg thought.

"What's cooking?" the man asked again, nodding to the cast-iron pot hanging over the campfire.

Jabeg shrugged. "Porridge, with biscuits. And a little bit of cheese."

"I've got some more cheese, and a few apples as well," said the stranger. He reached into his scrip and tossed Jabeg something round. For a fleeting instant, Jabeg's heart leaped into his throat. He caught it instinctively, though, and found it was just an apple.

"There's plenty more where that came from," said the stranger as he sat down carefully on the edge of a large stone. "I could use some warm porridge, though."

"Go ahead," said Jabeg softly, holding the apple with a vice-like grip. He decided that if the stranger tried to leave, he would have to kill him. Though the man cultivated an air of friendly congeniality, the glint in his eyes showed that he was not stupid.

"How old were you when you killed your first man?"

The question, like the apple toss, caught Jabeg by surprise. He narrowed his eyes as he considered how best to respond. The wind whistled over the rocky, treeless plateau, while on the southern horizon, the mighty Kevona mountains stood like hoary headed warriors lined for battle.

"What makes you think I've killed a man?"

"Because you're traveling the high road to Kevsura, alone. If you haven't killed a man before coming to these parts, then by now you certainly must have to survive so long."

Jabeg raised an eyebrow. *Does that include you, stranger?*

"I killed my first man when I was a boy," he answered, using his dagger to carve the apple. "It was the year of the long winter. I hadn't yet grown my beard."

"That young, eh?" said the stranger. He withdrew a wooden bowl and helped himself to the porridge. "It was the same with me. I grew up in a village by the seashore. My father was a blacksmith and made swords for the king's armies. One day, a baron from one of the neighboring cities came to commission a sword. My father made it exactly to the specifications, but when the baron refused to pay, he refused to give it to him. The baron then seized the weapon by force and struck my father down."

The stranger paused in his story. Behind him, the sun dipped low on the western horizon, painting the snow-capped peaks in crimson shades.

"When I saw what had happened, I challenged the baron to a duel. He laughed and sent his shield bearer to teach me a lesson. But my father had trained me well. I frightened the bearer's horse and slew him as he fell to the ground."

"So you're an outlaw, then?"

The stranger scowled. "When thieves and murderers make the laws, how can a man keep his honor and not become a criminal? The baron sent his men after me, so I fled into the wilderness. In time, I met others who had also suffered injustice."

Jabeg nodded, careful to maintain an awareness of his surroundings. If the man was supposed to distract him while his friends moved to attack, their plans would be sorely disappointed.

"What about yourself?" the stranger asked.

Jabeg ate a single apple slice, his dagger still in his hands. His senses were so heightened that the sweetness practically exploded in his mouth.

"I come from those mountains," he said, nodding to the line of snow-capped peaks. Though the shadows of twilight had settled across the campsite, the mountains still shone bright in the light of the setting sun.

The stranger pulled out some cheese and stirred it into the porridge. "Go on."

"In the mountains," Jabeg continued, "the laws are handed down to us by tradition, not the petty whims of lords or barons. My sister was raped by a young man in a neighboring clan. I was just a boy, but I slew him while he was working in the fields, together with two of his friends."

"You killed three men as a young boy?"

"Aye—though in truth, they were all cowards who would rather run than fight. I struck the last of them in the back as he fled. If they had stood against me like men, the outcome would have been very different."

"So what did you do afterwards?"

Jabeg sighed. "Because I had killed three men, I had incurred a debt of blood that could not be ignored. To prevent a feud war, my clan married my sister to her rapist's brother and threw me out as an exile. My sister gave birth to a son and killed herself shortly after."

"A bitter story," said the stranger. "Bitter stories for bitter times, eh?"

Jabeg didn't answer.

The wind grew stronger as the sky grew darker. Jabeg resisted the urge to throw more fuel on the fire, knowing that on the bare, stony ground of the Kevonan foothills, the light would mark the position of their camp for miles. Instead, he let the embers slowly die, pulling on his cloak to stave off the stiff wind. The stranger did the same.

"What is your name?" asked the stranger.

"My name is for my friends."

The stranger nodded slowly. "You are a cautious man."

"It is a trait that has served me well."

Off to the right, the grass rustled. Jabeg's heartbeat quickened as the crickets stopped singing. His had slowly slipped to the knife in his boot.

"Did you hear something behind me?" the stranger asked.

"What?"

"If I'm not mistaken, they're surrounding us as we speak," he said in a calm, unhurried tone. "How quickly can you get to your sword?"

Jabeg frowned. "I—"

"The moment we stop talking is the moment they strike. Are you ready?"

Sweat trickled down the front of Jabeg's face. He leaned forward, resting his weight on the balls of his feet.

Is he lying?

"I'm ready," he said softly. The dying embers glowed red, causing the twilight shadows to dance.

The sound of small rocks clattering made him dive for the ground. He rolled, and an arrow whistled past him. The stranger rose and drew his longsword, while Jabeg spun and threw the knife in the direction indicated by the arrow. A scream in the darkness was followed by the shouts of at least a dozen warriors.

Jabeg wasted no time. He ran to his pack and grabbed his scabbard just as movement blurred to his left. With the sword still sheathed, he blocked a heavy blow that sent him stumbling. The shouting was everywhere now, behind him and in front. The ringing clash of blades told him that the stranger was already engaged in the work of death.

Another blur, this one to his right. He blocked a blow with the scabbard, ducked beneath the second and quickly drew the blade. Before his attacker could recover, he plunged the sword deep into his stomach, twisting it once and grabbing the man by the throat. His dark eyes bulged in shock as Jabeg used his body to shield the next attack. Two blows struck the man's back with the same dull thud of an ax striking a tree— his comrades were either slow or stupid, or perhaps a little of both. Jabeg grinned.

"To me!" shouted the stranger, a hint of desperation in his voice. The ringing clash of steel sounded off to Jabeg's rear. Wrenching his sword free, he leaped and parried a blow before sending a riposte through his attacker's throat. The young bandit gurgled and fell to the ground, choking on his own blood.

"I'm here," said Jabeg, risking only a brief glance to confirm that the stranger was indeed behind him. "Keep your back to me, and—"

An arrow shot past his ear, nicking his skin and making his arm spasm. Was that a second archer, or had he failed to kill the first? He parried another blow and forced the attacker back before dropping to his knee.

"Turn right!" he shouted. Switching his sword to a reverse grip sinister, he retrieved the second throwing knife and spring to his feet. He deflected a blow and caught sight of a figure standing on a boulder above them. The throwing knife left his hand, spinning through the air. Moments later, the archer toppled backward without a sound, his bow clattering on the rocks.

As quickly as it had begun, the attack ceased. The few remaining bandits melted into the shadows like frightened strays. Jabeg pursued and slew two of them just a few short paces from the camp, while the stranger chased another in the opposite direction. A cry cut short by the sound of steel plunging into flesh told him that the stranger's blade had struck true.

Jabeg's hands shook and his knees quivered, but long practice in the craft of war had taught him mastery over his own nerves. He drew a long breath and wiped his sword clean on the shirt of the nearest dead bandit, mentally taking inventory of himself. His arms, his legs—everything seemed fine. His ear was scratched and a thin trickle of blood traced a path down the back of his neck, but the wound was inconsequential. He was alive.

How many did we kill? he wondered, surveying the scene. The sky was fully dark and the moon had not yet risen, so it was difficult to count the bodies—and harder still to recover his knives. At least half a dozen dead or dying men lay between him and the fire. Their groans grew fainter until there was nothing but the cold, empty stillness of death.

"We'll have to move camp," said the stranger, breaking the terrible silence. He walked up to Jabeg and sheathed his sword. "The wolves will be here as soon as they smell the blood, and that won't be too much longer."

He could have killed me, Jabeg realized. *With my back to him, the opportunity was his.*

"You fight well, stranger," he said. "I am indebted to you."

"As am I, which makes both our debts fully paid."

Jabeg chuckled and extended his hand. "My name is Jabeg. What's yours, friend?"

"Lucca Argonadze."

They clasped arms and turned to the task of breaking camp. Far off toward the snow-capped mountains, a wolf began to howl.

MEMOIRS OF A SNOWFLAKE

In the moment before my first memory, I feel a wonderful lightness, a floating sensation that isn't truly a sensation because I don't yet know who I am or that I am. But then I feel a coming together, a sense of going that is my becoming, my awakening. And that is my first memory.

I feel completely insubstantial as I float in a sea of white. It feels comforting and peaceful, like home. Childlike curiosity drives me to explore myself, and I find that my body is growing. Delicate tendrils of ice spread out in beautiful, unique patterns from the tiny part of me that was my beginning. I take joy and fascination in becoming aware of myself.

I feel the presence of many brothers and sisters. We are all growing, all newly self-aware. The whiteness takes form, too—she is our cloud-mother, and her presence fills our budding awareness. We are hers and feel at home in her.

You are growing very well, she tells us. *Soon it will be time to leave for the world below.*

We are afraid to leave her because she is our home, our mother. If we leave her, we will die. We don't know how we know this, but we do.

Don't be afraid, she tells us. *Every end is a beginning. You lived before you were born to me and you will return here after your time below is through. Every death gives way to a new rebirth.*

The words of our mother-cloud comfort us and help us forget our fears.

The time comes. We begin our gradual descent together, drifting slowly downward into the night. Staying close together helps us not to be afraid. Soon, our mother is far above us, still bidding us farewell.

When she is gone, we are alone in a sea of white. It is silent all around us. To lift the silence some of us begin to sing silent songs of thoughts, songs that we can all hear together in our minds. We sing of our mother and our brothers and sisters, of our anticipation for the world awaiting us below. Though we all share the same fears and anxieties, our individual thoughts and feelings are as unique as our crystalline bodies, and each of us adds something different to the thought-song to make it rich and beautiful. Soon, we feel confident and happy in ourselves. We miss our mother, but we are ready and excited to begin our lives in the world below.

After a little more time, we begin to see shapes in the murky whiteness: outlines that gradually become clearer and more distinct as we continue our descent. We see lights and shadows, shades of reddish-grey, and great lumbering shapes moving across the white-washed surface of the world.

We sense the additional presence of millions and millions more of our brothers and sisters. They are the ones who came before us. We greet them and ask how they are doing.

Some of them return our greetings and welcome us with great joy. They say that they are quite comfortable and have been doing very well. They describe the new world to us, a world of trees and streets, cars and people, things we have never known while living and growing with our cloud-mother. Their words fill us with wonder, and we look about for the things they described, though it is difficult to see anything clearly. The noises, too, are muffled and unfamiliar.

Others reply that we shouldn't think too much on the strange new things of this world. *When we arrived we had a good view for a short time,* they say, *but soon we were covered by others until we couldn't see anything. But there is nothing to fear. It is quite cozy and comfortable, and you will never feel alone.*

Others, though, give us dire warnings.

Watch out! they say. *Take care! These humans are not harmless creatures. They step all over us and crush our beautiful bodies into oblivion. And heaven help you if you land in the street! If you do, you will die in a mess of sludge and oil and grime.*

Their words frighten us and remind us of the death that awaits us. Some of us wish they had never come, and long to return to our cloud-mother where such pain was unknown.

Others from below treat us as if we are mere children.

Just wait, they say. *When the cloud-mother stops sending her children and the sun rises bright and terrible in the sky, you will hear the slow sounds of death and waste away in a sea of unpleasant, warm monotony. If you don't die, you will each merge together until your bodies become one sheet of transparent glass. In this way, your days will drag out until you melt into death, utterly forgotten.*

Many of us don't know what to think of these words. I don't know what to make of them. The fear I had before of leaving my cloud-mother comes back, making me feel helpless, and for a brief moment I panic, wishing I had never come down.

But then I remember her words. *Every end is a beginning. You lived before you were born to me and you will return here after your time below is through. Every death gives way to a new rebirth.*

I will not end. I have not ended. I have lived before and will live again—I will not be erased or eradicated. Even if I lose my individuality, in my rebirth I will again rise unique.

I look down and see a figure below me: a human, smaller than the others. She sticks out her tongue to catch me, but as I fall slowly towards her waiting mouth, I am not afraid.

THE CURSE OF THE LIFEWALKER

My given name is Isaac Jameson, but most people know me as the Lifewalker. It is a fitting title. In a world where few men live to the age of twenty five, I wander the Earth alone, watching each generation spring up, bear seed, and pass away with the autumn frost. Yet with each new crop of humanity, death refuses to harvest me. I am truly a stranger in my own homeland, a man washed up on the shores of time. There are some who would view these many long years of life as a blessing. Indeed, before the Blight, the natural lifespan of man was many times longer than it is today. But when all the world is afflicted by the plague, sometimes the greater curse is to be whole.

I was born in a small farming commune in the south of the land of Provorem, a peaceful region nestled in the mountains of the west. It lies in a wide valley with a shallow freshwater lake at its center. It is a good place for catfish and mussels, as well as heron and other waterfowl. The mountains rise sharply all around it, but more especially to the east, though none boast a peak that is snow-capped year round. A monument to the letter Y can still been seen on the face of one of the nearer foothills, though the coloring has long since faded. The northeast border of the valley is guarded by a mountain that carries the ancient name of Timpanogos. It has the appearance of a young maiden, sleeping on her back with a hand on her pregnant belly. Some say that the child she carries is the hope of the new world.

As the first child to my young parents, I was blessed to know them before they died. My father was a man of the land. He taught me how to till the earth and read the seasons, how to build a house, and how to hunt for wild game to keep the commune well-fed. He was also something of a tinker, though his skills were more mechanically inclined and not suited to electronic artifacts. In my eighth year, he helped me build my first bicycle, with wooden tires and saddlebags sewn from buckskin.

My mother was from a journeyman commune on the north side of Provorem, among the ruins of the city. From her, I learned the timeless and invaluable skill of reading. Through the small collection of books which she gave me, my eyes were first opened to the world beyond our humble commune. My collection included an old, battered dictionary, the Holy Scriptures, and a fantasy adventure titled *Mistborn: The Final Empire.* As a child, I read every scrap of paper I could find, digging through old ruins just to find a waterlogged tome or two. Of course, most of these had already been gathered for safekeeping at the Great Library, so at the end of my twelfth year, I petitioned the commune to allow me to enroll and begin my studies.

The Great Library of Provorem is one of the more famous institutions in all of the mountains of the west. Before the Blight, it was a great place of learning, where scholars came from all over the world to study and acquire knowledge. A small group of them managed to preserve the collection from the worst of the times of trouble, and students from all the surrounding valleys come there to study to this day. A few of the original structures have fallen into disrepair, but many of them still stand, thanks to the journeyman communes who have made those ruins their home.

For one joy-filled year, I devoted all of my time to my studies. I read about the great American nation that had once stretched from ocean to ocean, filling the face of the whole continent. I read about the magic and wonders of the past, when people traveled in the bellies of enormous flying machines, and spoke to each other from across the world as easily as if they were sitting in the same room. So great were the marvels unfolded to my view that I felt to stand in awe beneath a mighty waterfall of pure knowledge.

Sadly, my days at the Great Library ended almost before they had a chance to begin. My mother took ill with the Blight in the ninth month of my studies, and her condition rapidly worsened. Before the end of the winter, she passed away. My father was inconsolable, and requested that I return to the commune of my birth, though my two younger sisters were still living at home with him. Perhaps he saw that his own days were numbered. It crushed my young heart to leave my studies behind, but I honored his wishes and returned.

I spent a year at home, working the land of our commune by father's side. This was a year of great changes, when the things I had read began to stir a great restlessness within me. My wanderings and explorations, which before had been limited to the ruins of Provorem, now began to range further afield. I began to climb the mountains immediately around our valley, on the pretense of hunting game. In reality, though, I was stretching myself, pushing back against the boundaries that confined my little world.

On the south end of the lake, within sight of the land of my birth, stands a small mountain with a bald top. Near the summit, a red and white tower from the days before the Blight still rises like a spear into the sky. The purpose of the tower has long been forgotten, though some tinkers claim that these towers were used by the forefathers to talk with the stars.

In the summer of my fourteenth year, I determined to climb that mountain and explore their ruins for myself. The trail, though steep and winding, traced a wide path up the northern face. The day I selected was warm and sunny, and the sky was perfectly clear, offering a wonderful view of the valley on either side. A pleasant breeze put me in high spirits, and in just an hour, I reached the tower's base.

While exploring the ruins, I noticed a small, curious structure on the west side of the mountain. A large white dome extended like a bubble over the roof, with two smaller domes on the farther side. When I approached the structure to investigate, I noticed a small vegetable garden, with an empty cowpen in the back. The footpath leading up to the place was not very worn. I approached it cautiously, not knowing who lived there.

When I was within twenty yards, a man stepped out of the door and waved a small cane at me.

"Well, don't just stand there," he said. "Come in or be on your way."

I stared speechless at him for some time. Unlike the people in my commune—or indeed, in any commune that I had encountered in the whole of Provorem—his hair was as white as new-fallen snow, with a long, grizzled beard extending from his chin. Wrinkles lined his brow, while his back was slightly bent, so that he needed a cane to walk.

In short, he was unlike anyone I had ever seen.

"Well?" he said again, raising his voice over the mountain breeze. "Are you coming in or aren't you?"

I accepted his invitation, and over a light lunch of potatoes, cheese, and sliced tomatoes, we soon became good friends. Adam, as he called himself, had grown up in one of the northern communes of Provorem, between the lake and the Great Library. The Blight had taken his parents while he was still young, so he left the commune when he was ten and became an apprentice to the curator. Like me, his thirst for knowledge was unquenchable. He read as many of the books as he could get his hand on, including some of the same ones that I had. When the Blight took his master, Adam succeeded him as the new curator.

For ten years, he worked tirelessly to preserve and expand the Great Library's collection. He even declined to marry, considering his work more important than raising a family. However, when he reached the end of his twenty-fifth year, he did not sicken or grow pale. The Blight refused to take him, and as the years rolled on it became clear that he was destined to live.

At first, he saw this as a great blessing—a chance to continue his life's work without the untimely interruption of death. However, the other scholars at the Great Library soon became wary of him. When it became clear that the Blight would not take him, his apprentices did all they could to oust him. Recognizing that a political struggle would only harm the institution in the long run, he stepped down from his position as curator and exiled himself to the mountain. There, he had decided to live out the remainder of his days alone, returning to the valley only occasionally to trade for food and supplies.

When I asked why he had chosen such a lonely life of solitude, he didn't answer me, but instead insisted that I remain for the night. The domes, he explained, were telescopes—mechanical eyes that could see into the heavens. Since I had no pressing duties at the commune for the next few days, I accepted his invitation and helped him with his chores until the sun set across the lake and the moon rose through the clefts in the mountains.

"On a moonless night," he told me, "you can observe the stars more properly, but the moon is worth observing of itself."

He took me to the heart of the structure and turned a crank that opened the dome overhead. By wheeling a set of mirrors over a large turntable, we moved the machine into position so that it was pointing directly at the moon. When we were finished, he took me to the eyepiece and had me look into it.

To my astonishment, I beheld a stunning gray landscape full of mountains, valleys, and dark, flat plains. Giant circles covered the land—craters, or in other words, as Adam informed me, the impact of collisions with other celestial objects. The ancients had called the plains *mares,* because they had the appearance of wide, tranquil seas. As I stared at them, the sight so entranced me that I could barely speak.

"You know," said Adam, "before the days of the Blight, there were men who traveled to the moon and walked on it."

"What?" I said, looking up sharply. "That's impossible!"

"It's not impossible," he said with a smile. "I should know—I was the chief curator, after all."

"But—but how?"

He shrugged. "We no longer have the means to fully comprehend the mechanics of how they did it. However, that does not change the fact that they did. Somewhere up there, on the face of our moon, you will find the footprints of men."

I stared at the moon in wonder for several moments. The very idea so entranced me that for many days I could think of nothing else. Suddenly, the boundaries between communes seemed tediously small, the mountains no longer the end of my world but the beginning of it. I spent hours planning elaborate trips to the far side of the valley, and climbed all the major peaks within sight of my home. Beyond each mountain, there was always another valley, and another mountain and another valley beyond that.

If I had set out at that time to wander the Earth, my life would have taken a much different course. The zealousness of youth often propels us to make reckless decisions, which we later come to regret. In this forlorn age of the Blight, most of our lives are cut short before we can fully experience this. As the Lifewalker, though, I have come to learn that regrets can be as deadly as poison—even worse, for they sap the spirit, without which the body is but an empty shell.

With my father in his final years, I reluctantly agreed to postpone my travels at least until after his passing. The elders of the commune, seeing my eagerness to set out on my own, conspired to find some way to keep me.

In retrospect, their strategy was obvious. My childish body had already begun to change, my voice low and the shadow of a beard spreading across my chin. I spent much more time in the company of the girls my age than I had only the year before. The elders saw this, and arranged for my betrothal to a young girl named Lydia from a neighboring commune.

At first, I was incensed. I wanted to see the world—what use to me was a wife? As soon as I laid eyes on her, though, my anger soon cooled. The women of the mountains are famous for their beauty, but none of them could compare to my Lydia. Her hair was as golden as the sun, her eyes as blue as a clear summer sky. Her skin was as smooth as the stones of the river, her lips as cool and refreshing as a high mountain stream. As we spent more and more time together, my heart stirred until I could not bear to be separated from her. She was kind and patient, and listened with great interest to all my hopes and dreams. After only a few months, I don't think we had a single secret between us.

"It's so frustrating," I told her one day, as we sat together on the riverbank not far from the lake shore. "If men in the old times could travel as far as the moon, why should I stay here in this valley?"

"What's on the moon that's so interesting?" she asked, holding my hand. I picked up a stone and skipped it across the water.

"I don't know," I admitted. "Just—more than this."

"If no one lives up there, it must be a lonely place. I wouldn't ever want to go there."

"Why not?"

She shrugged, though in her eyes, I could see a great weight of emotion, perhaps even fear. She turned to face me.

"Isaac," she said, "if it came between me or the world, which would you choose?"

I was dumbfounded. In my youthful naiveté, I had never seen it as a choice I would have to make. Until that point, life had been something that had happened to me, not something over which I had any significant control. The elders in the commune made all of the major decisions, and I went along with them willingly or not. But looking in her eyes, I realized that I did have a choice—and that that choice would not only impact my own life, but hers as well.

"I—I don't know," I stammered. "Couldn't you just come with me? We could travel the world together. Think about it!"

She bit her lip and looked away. "But Isaac, my home is here."

My heart fell as I realized she would never leave the valley. Still, in my youthful stubbornness, I was determined to do all I could to fight against the pull of home.

"Home," I sneered. "What's so great about that anyway? Have you ever climbed any of those mountains? From the top, you can look down and see half a dozen valleys just like ours, stretching all the way to the horizon."

She squeezed my hand, but I ignored it.

"Don't you ever get bored of this place?" I asked. "Don't you ever look at the ruins around this valley and ask yourself about the people who built them? Before the days of the Blight, our fathers had flying machines that could take them around the world. They each had a magic seer stone that could bring all the books of the Great Library into the palms of their hands."

"Not all miracles have passed away," she said softly, dipping her bare toes into the water. "The greatest wonders are still here with us."

I frowned. "How do you mean?"

"Have you ever seen the birth of an infant, or watched a child take its first step? Those are miracles, too. And isn't it adventure enough just to have children? To settle down and make a home with the one you love?"

I shook my head. "There's got to be something more out there, Lydia. Something out there is calling to me. I have to answer it."

"And spend the rest of your life childless and alone?"

"I—"

She squeezed my hand again, more firmly this time. "We weren't meant to wander this world by ourselves, Isaac. We need each other."

"But—but I'm in my fifteenth year!" I said, oblivious to her advances. "In another ten years, the Blight will take me. How can I afford to settle down now?"

"How can you afford not to?"

She leaned in close, and I realized that I would never leave her. I lifted my hand to her cheek, and we kissed beneath the shady willows along the riverbank.

We were married the following spring, just after the last frost of the season. The Blight took my father less than a month later, but at least he died with the satisfaction of knowing that his only son had taken a wife. It was a time of many changes, but we braved it as well as we could by staying close to our community. Lydia was always there for me, offering her consolation in moments of private grief. Our love waxed stronger with each passing day. We were truly inseparable.

For a brief time, all my dreams of wandering the earth departed. We lived each day in the present, and I can honestly say it was the happiest time of my life.

But happiness always carries a bittersweet edge. Though Lydia's greatest desire was to become a mother, we were never blessed with children. One year passed after another, and yet our marriage remained childless. Now it was my turn to console her as she had consoled me, except that her grief far exceeded my own.

I will always remember those nights in which she cried herself to sleep in my arms, trembling for fear that her time was rapidly coming to an end. And indeed it was—the Blight had already taken almost all of the elders of the commune, leaving many late-born orphans. We did our best to care for them, which gave her no small degree of comfort and delight. In the autumn of her life, she was known as the commune's mother, and dearly loved by all.

Yet just as autumn turns to winter, so too did our time together come to an end.

In the twenty-fourth year of her life, Lydia contracted a cold which soon turned into pneumonia. As her cheeks paled and her limbs grew weak, I realized that the Blight was taking her. I did all I could to ease her passing, but my grief as she slipped beyond my capacity to care for her was the greatest sorrow I have ever felt in my long life. When her spirit finally passed beyond this world, I collapsed on the earth and wept bitterly. I had never felt so alone.

A year passed, and then another. The council of elders now consisted entirely of my peers. Both of my sisters joined the council, taking care of the late-born orphans in Lydia's absence. And yet, even though my time had come and gone, I felt no weakness, but remained healthy and strong.

As my first sister paled and took sick with the Blight, I realized with an awful finality that I would soon outlive them both. I cannot possibly convey in words the terror that this realization gave me. It had been bad enough to watch my beloved Lydia pass away in my arms. To do the same with each of my sisters—and indeed, with all of my closest friends—it was almost more than I could bear.

For the next two years, I fell into a dark depression, worse than any I have felt before or after. I do not remember how I made it through these times, but after the passing of my last sister, I was finally and truly alone. Everyone I had ever looked up to had passed away.

At the close of my twenty-eighth year, as the days began to shorten in anticipation of the coming harvest, I decided that I couldn't possibly spend one more winter in this place that filled me with constant sorrow. I determined to set out immediately after the harvest, leaving the commune behind forever. That no one tried to stop me was a testament in itself that I no longer belonged.

On the tenth day of the ninth month, thirteen days before my thirtieth birthday, I left the place of my birth for the last time. I packed my father's old books, a heavy wool blanket, a single change of clothes, an assortment of pans and cooking utensils, two weeks' worth of food, a hunting knife, and a small bow with a quiver full of arrows. All these I placed carefully in a small trailer which I attached to the back of my bicycle.

On my way south out of the land of Provorem, I made one last trek to the summit of the lone mountain. I found Adam tending his garden, his back more hunched and his hands shaking worse than remembered.

"Are you doing all right?" I asked him. "That's mighty hard work for an old man."

"Yes, but it's my work," he answered in a quavering voice. "And this is my place, where I belong."

I looked into his face and saw the same sorrow that had, for the past several years, consumed me. In that moment, I realized exactly why Adam had chosen to exile himself so far from human company. He narrowed his eyes at me.

"You have it too, don't you?"

"Yes," I answered, swallowing a little. Though I did not explain the purpose of my visit, we both knew that I had come to say goodbye.

Adam nodded and leaned heavily on his shovel. "I suppose you won't be staying long."

"No. I'm leaving Provorem."

"Well," he said, coughing, "In that case, I expect this visit will be our last."

I didn't have an answer. We shared a moment of companionable silence together. The waters of the lake shimmered in the light of the late-afternoon sun, and the golden-brown grass of the mountainside swayed in the stiff mountain breeze. The white domes of the aging telescopes stood like sentinels against the inexorable passage of time, the whistling of the wind an echo of the emptiness in my own lonely heart. When I had come here before, I had been filled with vague dreams of setting out to see the world. Now, though, it was not adventure that I sought, but solace. Each passing day sent me further into exile from all I had ever known.

"Strangers we are, wandering through a strange land," Adam muttered. "Take care of yourself, boy."

"I will."

"Don't expect the loneliness to get any better. It doesn't."

I choked back a tear and nodded.

"Still," he added, "you're young. You may not feel it, but you are. You have a long time still ahead of you."

"I know," I whispered. That was what I was afraid of.

We shared only a few brief moments before I turned my back on the land of my youth, never to behold it with my natural eyes again.

In the long and painful years since, I have often thought of Adam and his little hermitage on the lonely mountain. In my youth, I wondered why any man would choose to exile himself from his fellow men. But now, I know. In a world where death is as timely and unchanging as the seasons, the greater hardship is to live.

"Uh, sir, we have a situation."

Captain Jason12 frowned. "What kind of situation?"

"A girl situation, sir."

The captain sighed and leaned back in his command chair, while the fifty or so technicians on the bridge looked up anxiously from their posts. The soft glow of thousands of input feeds scrolled across the main display screen, barely illuminating the dark room with their shimmering letters and numbers. Jason12 drew in a deep breath.

"Optical Recon, report," Jason12 commanded.

"Yes, sir," answered one of the technicians. "Subject is female, brown hair, about five foot six, age estimated at eighteen to twenty two, approaching on foot at twelve o'clock sharp. Processing name and association."

"Bring it up onto the main screen and give us a live visual."

"Already processing, sir."

The numbers and letters scrolling across the main display screen blinked out, and the bridge became something of a giant theater, giving the captain and all the technicians in main cerebral the view from outside. Trees and red brick buildings came into view, under a blue sky with puffy white clouds. A large crowd of students walked across the college campus, packed in a tight, swirling mass off to the left but spread out more sparsely to the right.

Directly ahead and about ten yards away, a young brunette walked towards the viewers. Her long, straight hair was pulled back in a ponytail, and her bright blue eyes had just started to turn upward. Judging from the female's movements as processed through Optical Reconnaissance, though, it didn't appear to Jason12 that she'd identified them yet.

The events on screen advanced in slow motion, about twelve microseconds measured externally for every second measured internally on the bridge. That was real time for Jason12 and his men aboard the *Chris Murray.*

"Captain, association determination is complete," said the technician at optical. "Subject identified as the *Michelle Walker.*"

A short collective gasp escaped from the captain's men. Jason12 clenched his teeth together slightly.

"Association identified as classmate, friend, and secret crush of the *Chris Murray,*" continued the technician at optical. "I have a reference on file here to the decisions queue, line LZ1527."

"Captain!" shouted one of the technicians overseeing the core reactor complex behind the bridge, "I'm picking up a series of new fluctuations in the emotions matrix!"

Of course, thought Jason12. After all, every system on main cerebral automatically fed into the core. Jason12 was captain of the *Chris Murray* in name, but all the truly meaningful decisions were made somewhere inside the mysterious inner core.

"What sort of fluctuations are you reading?" he asked.

"It's too mixed to say, but we're getting a lot of them. Excitement, attraction, desire, self-consciousness, and about twenty other unidentified frequencies. At the current rate of acceleration, the matrix will blow in just under twenty milliseconds."

"Reroute the energy overflow to the solar plexus." That would give the *Chris Murray* instability in the stomach and the upper intestinal tract, but the Emotions matrix would hold. A fairly standard procedure.

"Sir! I'm getting a new command from the core."

"Put it on the main display."

A line of command code text superimposed itself over the video feed from outside. It read:

```
:open(upper.memory.log);
:search122=blank;
:set.search.term(search122)="michelle walker";
:execute(search122);
```

So far, things were proceeding exactly the way they had the last time they had encountered the

Michelle Walker. Now was the time for some creative thinking—but nothing was coming to Jason12.

"Feed the core the memory file associated with the line in the decisions queue. We're not going to let the inner core forget that decision."

The captain walked to the motor skills section of the bridge. "How long before we reach expected verbal communication range with the subject?" he asked the technician in charge of the subunit.

"I'd say perhaps nineteen hundred milliseconds, give or take fifty."

"Not much time."

"Attention, captain," came a voice over the loudspeaker, "this is optical processing. We have established eye contact with the subject. She has returned contact and appears to have a reading on us."

Sure enough, on the main screen, the female's bright blue eyes had turned up. A smile spread across her face in slow motion.

"Sir," cried a technician back at the matrices, "I have a new fluctuation in the emotions matrix. It's spiraling out of control!"

"What is it now?"

"We have a new frequency and it's blowing up fast. It appears to be a sharp dose of fear."

The captain stomped his foot in frustration and cursed. "Great Anencephaly!"

"The emotions matrix is overflowing. It's overflowing!"

"Begin adrenaline pump. Give us a sharp jolt and maintain at thirty percent."

"Initiating adrenaline surge, sir."

The captain clenched his hand into a tight fist. Though the inner core of the *Chris Murray* had quite a positive association with the *Michelle Walker,* there was still a very real barrier of fear that needed to be brought down in order to execute the decisions queue. It was going to take a large dose of courage to overcome the fear barrier and execute the crucial decision— courage that the systems aboard the *Chris Murray* simply couldn't muster in the 1600 milliseconds before expected verbal contact.

"It's too late," cried the matrix technician. "We have overflow into the Cognative matrix. It's short circuiting the logs and freezing everything!"

"Schizoid!" Jason12 cursed.

With the Cognative matrix frozen, he knew that no amount of thinking would bring the *Chris Murray* to execute the decisions queue. In fact, the thinking only served to prolong hesitancy. And since the emotions matrix was so unstable, an appeal to emotions would probably bring a flight response, hardly something conducive to the situation. Main cerebral would have to issue the command itself—and main cerebral was unable to issue the necessary commands without assistance from the matrices.

Jason12 didn't know how he was going to get out of this one. The last time this had happened, the previous captain had been demoted. He had to do something, but what?

At that moment, a brilliant idea flashed into his mind. The necessary assistance didn't *have* to come through the matrices, if he could somehow override the matrix interface...

"Alright, men!" said captain Jason12, "I want a direct command line to the inner core. We need to get the *Chris Murray* to stop thinking and just take action."

"But captain, you know the protocols. We can't—"

"Yes we can. Disconnect the main command console from the Cognative matrix and wire it into the subconscious download interface. We can begin the command line by splicing it with a line from the memory matrix, since the memory already feeds directly into the subconscious. Once we get a positive response from the core, we'll hack it from there. Bring up the memory feed on my main console."

"Yes, sir! What label conditions should we set?"

"Give me search results from the philosophy section only, with search terms 'act,' 'think,' and 'do.' "

"Beginning search."

The captain sat down at his command console. A tremendous jumble of raw data flew across the screen, but his mind instantly made sense of it all. He set his face against the screen and furiously searched through the data for the code he needed.

"ETA?" asked the captain without taking his eyes off the screen.

"Nine hundred milliseconds and counting," called out the technician at optical.

The captain worked faster. After only a few seconds, his eyes lit up with recognition. He isolated the data, brought up the code, and turned to the nearest group of technicians.

"Alright, I want a command line brought up and spliced with this line of code right here." said Jason12. He turned to the matrix technician. "And I want a direct wiring link established between my console and the core!"

"I'm on it!" said the technician. He'd already sent in a few of his men behind the glass to rewire the matrices. They worked frantically to rebuild the system, surrounded by switchboards and tangled masses of unplugged cords.

"Out of curiosity," said the matrix technician as the men behind the glass finished their work, "what's the memory file we're splicing?"

"It's a quote from Winston Churchill."

"Line established," called out the technician from behind the glass. He had just finished rewiring the interface.

"Very good," said the captain, "let's get that command line spliced."

"It's done."

"Excellent. Begin direct feed."

A quotation came up on the main console. It had been taken directly from the memory matrix, and read:

I never worry about action, but only inaction.

"What now?" called out one of the junior technicians.

"Now," said the captain, "we wait for a response from the core."

The milliseconds ticked down slowly. On the main display, the *Michelle Walker* drew closer. Eye contact was still holding, and she appeared to be initiating a smile.

"ETA?" called out the captain.

"Two hundred milliseconds."

"Captain, captain!" called out the matrix technician, "I'm receiving a response from the core!"

"Superimpose it on the main display."

"Rerouting through Cognitive matrix."

A new command came up. It read:

```
:think!=good;
:instinct==good;
:execute(good);
```

A shout came up from the technicians on the bridge. "We have direct command line established! Repeat, we have direct command line established!"

"Excellent work, men!" said Jason12. Now, with the direct command line, he could prompt the inner core without having to go through the already over-loaded Cognative and Emotions matrices.

"Captain, we're receiving a verbal signal from the subject. Processing raw data feed from main auditory."

"Process it quickly."

A few more milliseconds passed. After a brief wait, it came up on the main display, with an audio replay in synced time.

Hi Chris!

It was exactly as Jason12 had expected. He already was typing in a prompt through the direct command line. When it was finished, he hit enter and sent the feed directly to the inner core. Now he'd find out just how strong that direct line really was.

"ETA is zero. We are within expected window of verbal communication."

"Captain, I'm receiving a new command from the core. It's responding to your prompt!"

"What's the command?" asked the captain.

"I'm reading multiple commands for the Gustation and Motor systems, with verbal line *:system.out.speakln("hey Michelle!");*"

The direct line prompt had worked. The *Chris Murray* wasn't acting on thoughts or emotions alone, but on 'gut feelings.' The feelings weren't really coming from the lower abdomen, however—they were coming from main cerebral. From captain Jason12 and his men.

"Excecute the command."

The captain watched the main display as the verbal signal transmitted. The *Michelle Walker* came to a stop.

"How is the emotions matrix holding?" called out the captain.

"I don't know! I'm getting a lot of mixed signals! The system is still very unstable!"

"Increase adrenaline to forty percent and lockdown Cognative and Emotions matrices. I don't want any interference from either one to botch up this operation!"

"Acknowledged."

"Receiving auditory signal from subject!"

"Process and display it on the main display," said the captain.

A new line came up on the screen, superimposed over the image of the *Michelle Walker.*

Yes?

Jason12 smiled. He knew what to do from here. He performed the splice himself and sent in the prompt through the direct command line.

A couple of milliseconds passed. The tension in the room was growing. The feed to the core had been quite large that last time, and timing was everything now.

"Sir," said the matrix technician, "I'm receiving a new command from the core."

"Send it up."

He read the command quickly. It was quite large—larger than he'd expected it to be. As he read it, he allowed a smile to spread across his face.

"Execute immediately!"

The command went from the main console out to the Gustation and Motor processing subunits. The technicians worked furiously at their stations to translate the prompt into raw nerve signals that the various muscular units could execute. They worked quickly and efficiently, and despite the breakdown of both the Cognative and Emotions matrices, the *Chris Murray* executed the full action as it had been relayed to them.

Hey, Michelle, I heard about this great new exhibit at the Springville art museum this weekend, and I was wondering if you wanted to go there with me this Saturday?

There was a long wait. Main Cerebral was utterly silent. The captain closed his eyes and took in a deep breath. The other technicians tried to find tedious things to do to pass the time.

"Receiving a new feed from Auditory."

"Process it and display."

After some time, a message flashed across the screen.

What time?

"Emotions matrix is destabilizing!"

"Great Anencephaly! Increase the adrenaline and make sure she holds."

"Receiving a new command from the core."

The captain read it and nodded. "Execute immediately."

Once again, the technicians furiously went to work. The time passed painfully slow until the vocal gustation unit sent out the auditory signal.

We'd probably leave around three o'clock, and stay for a couple of hours.

"Gustation complete."

"Captain, the emotions matrix is breaking down. We only have ninety milliseconds before we lose the direct command line."

Jason12 nodded grimly. He'd done all he could do, and now all they could do was wait. Still, at least he'd succeeded in executing decision LZ1527—the decision to ask Michelle out on a date this weekend.

But had the decision been executed well? Had it been executed with confidence? With feeling? Or had it come across as too mechanical, too awkward? Yes, they had technically executed the decision, but Jason12 might have botched it up after all. He'd made a risk in running the direct line—the inner core had simply been following prompts, not synthesizing an optimal response on its own. And no matter how much maneuvering they managed to do on main cerebral, they weren't capable of independently synthesizing all of the command sequences to transmit the interrogatory in the most optimal and effective manner. If the response from the *Michelle Walker* came back negative because of the awkward manner in which the *Chris Murray* had executed the interrogatory, there was more than a 50% chance of long term destabilization in the inner core. If that happened, then surely it would be the lower intestinal tract for Jason12.

The tension grew in the room with each millisecond. The technicians didn't speak. They just fidgeted tediously as they stared at the main display.

"Emotions matrix has overheated. Line broken!"

"Come on," murmured Jason12.

A few more milliseconds. The tension in the room kept growing and growing.

"Captain! Receiving new feed from Auditory! Processing it now!"

A new text superimposed itself over a smiling image of the *Michelle Walker.*

Yeah, that sounds like fun!

A loud cheer sounded across the bridge
"We did it! We did it!"

"Captain, we're receiving a new fluctuation in the emotions matrix. System is reversing polarity, repeat, reversing polarity!"

"Begin reduction of adrenaline flow and initiate endorphin release at 40% maximum."

"Acknowledged, Captain."

Amid the cheers and congratulations, Jason12 sat back down in his command chair. Communication between vessels continued, establishing minor details about the planned mutual encounter on Saturday, but these could be handled without hardly any trouble at all. He issued commands to reboot and clear the Cognative matrix, which would then restore normal interface with the core. The *Chris Murray* was stabilizing quickly and enjoying a huge rush of positive energy, and the technicians all shook hands and congratulated each other, anxiety giving way to triumph and relief.

Jason12 closed his eyes and sat back in his chair. What a day. But the real ride, he knew, would begin at three o'clock on Saturday.

Jane Carter of Earth and the Rescue that Never Was

In all her years at Earthfleet Academy, Jane Carter never thought she'd be the first human to be sold at an alien slave auction.

The door to her cell oscillated open, and two reptilian guards stepped in. As a certified xenologist, she wasn't supposed to see her captors as hideous, but there simply was no other way to describe them. Their wicked yellow claws and thick brown scales gave them the appearance of something from a medieval depiction of hell, and their horned faces only added to the effect. Jane grew tense the moment they strode inside.

"Hoo-man!" the first guard snarled in the local alien trade language. He poked at her with his assault rifle and motioned to the door.

Jane rose gracefully to her feet, preserving as much of her dignity as she could. The slavers certainly hadn't made it easy. Her hands and feet were chained, her neck firmly collared. In a previous escape attempt, she'd quickly found out that the chains were electrified. Her captors had stripped her naked, because of course they had. If there were any other humans at the auction, she would probably curl up and die.

No, she told herself. *Don't let them get the best of you.*

Fortunately, the odds of any humans attending the slave auction were low. In all of her travels of the Scutum-Crux galactic arm, the only other one she'd met was a certain Sam Kletchka, from the Gliese colony of New Texas.

Then again, he was the last person she wanted to see her like this.

The guards led her out into the hallway. The stone floor was uncomfortably rough on her bare feet. In the cell across from her, a group of tentacle-faced Setarni huddled in fear.

"Where are my things?" she asked.

"What things, hoo-man?"

"The things I had when you captured me. I'm a scientist; you'll make a bigger profit if you sell me as a specialist, not an exotic pet."

The guards laughed, a sound not unlike gargling broken glass.

"Foolish hoo-man! We make most profit selling you and your things separately."

Jane's heart sank. "You're making a mistake," she tried to argue, but a sharp shock to her neck convinced her to drop the matter.

They led her into a holding pen with tall, transparent walls. On the other side was an arena with an elevated platform to show off the merchandise. Every seat in the place was packed.

Jane scanned the crowd from her vantage point behind the gate. *Please don't be here, please don't be here...*

Ahead of her, the guards tore a Setarni child away from its mother. The mother let out a high pitched wail, her facial tentacles writhing in agony. When she tried to run after her child, though, the guards beat her down with their shock prods.

No!

None of this was ever supposed to happen. The Setarni had been part of a refugee convoy, fleeing the home system for the outlying colonies. They were supposed to be going somewhere safer, where she could continue her work in peace. But then the slavers had ambushed them, and their armed escort—including Sam—had betrayed them into the slavers' hands.

The crowd began to bid on the Setarni child. The bidding price flashed in real-time on half a dozen screens. From a purely xenological perspective, the auction was quite fascinating. The bidders held up batons that flashed a range of colors, probably signifying their bids. The balcony housed several private booths, each with a set of lights that flashed similar to the batons. It reminded her a bit of a Las Vegas casino, back home on Earth.

The lights flashed out one by one as a winning bid was reached. The mother fell to the rough stone floor, completely inconsolable.

"Next!" the announcer's voice bellowed over the loudspeakers. As he described the mother Setarni that the guards now dragged onto the platform, his words were translated into half a dozen galactic trade languages. Through the din, Jane made out at least three from the other end of the Scutum-Crux. This slave auction was huge.

As the lights blinked out one by one, she scanned the crowd more frantically. She was up next.

Had Sam been in on the plot to betray them? Jane wouldn't put it past him. He was a mercenary, free-lancing his way across the galaxy. Back at Earthfleet Academy, they'd dated each other a couple of times, but money and thrill-seeking were the only things he cared about, not serving humanity or paving the way for peaceful galactic relations. It was just as well that he'd dropped out before the end of her senior year. So would he leave her to the slavers just to swoop in and claim that he'd rescued her? Almost certainly.

Sam, if you win this auction, I'm going to give you such a piece of my mind...

The lights flashed out, and the gate swung open. The guards yanked on her chain, making her stumble as they forced her onto the platform. She was on.

"Last of all," the announcer called, "from the farthest side of the galaxy, and a planet of which few have ever told tale, we have a young female hoo-man!"

Nearly all of the lights flashed green and blue as the auctioning began. The announcer rattled off a host of "facts" about humans, most of them no more accurate than something out of *Gulliver's Travels* or *Baron*

Von Münchhausen. For Jane, however, the voice soon faded into the general din as crowd clamored all around her.

"Where are you, Sam?" she muttered under her breath. Her palms went clammy, and her heart started to race. She tried again to scan the crowd, but the lights were flashing too quickly for her to make out more than a few of the many bidders. Behind her, the numbers on the screens began to rise: eight million, nine million, ten million...

What if Sam wasn't there? What if she ended up in some sort of alien zoo—or worse, an inter-special harem? Panic seized her, making her throat constrict. This was more than just another interesting anthropological experience. It was real.

She glanced behind her at the numbers on the screens. What she saw made her cheeks go white. The bidding had cleared twenty million. That was enough to buy your own starship! All the Setarni in the convoy couldn't have gone for more than fifty. And yet the bidders showed no sign of stopping. If anything, their lights seemed to flash all the faster.

Did Sam have anything close to that kind of money? Was he panicking just as hard as she was?

The bidding cleared thirty million and quickly rose to forty. Jane's stomach fell—Forty million was enough in most systems to buy a luxury yacht. What kind of person would lay down that kind of money for a slave? It made her feel sick.

When the bidding passed fifty million, she felt like throwing up. There was absolutely no way Sam could buy her freedom now. He'd have to swoop in with guns blazing, killing the guards and taking out the automated defenses. The only escape was by teleporter, but the slavers doubtless had an interdiction field to prevent that very thing from happening. Maybe Sam was dealing with that now. After disabling the field, he'd burst into the hall, leap onto the platform, shoot all the guards and grab her. They'd teleport onto his ship, where she'd scream and cry and slap him for putting her through all this, and then kiss him for rescuing her. And maybe then she could finally put on some clothes.

"Please, Sam," she whispered, her voice trembling.

At fifty-eight million, the lights on the floor began to flicker out. By sixty-five million, only the anonymous patrons in the private booths were still bidding. But their lights showed no sign of slowing, and the bidding soon surpassed seventy million.

Jane lost all sensation in her legs. If she wasn't so terrified, she'd be laughing her head off. Seventy million—you could buy a small moon for that. Heck, she'd even heard of a planet selling for just under a hundred and twenty. Was she worth as much as a planet? She almost wanted to see.

The bidding passed eighty million, but the private bidders were starting to drop out. By eighty-two million, there were only three of them left. She looked up at the booths, wondering what kind of people were behind the glass. Kinky alien billionaires? Collectors of exotic life forms? Would she end up frozen in stasis on a display wall, like Han Solo from the original Star Wars series? Whoever they were, they were monsters to bring so much money to a slave auction. She didn't care how unprofessional that thought made her.

Not that it mattered anymore. Unless something incredible happened in the next few minutes, she would be a slave for the rest of her life. Her dreams of studying alien languages and becoming a renowned xenolinguist were falling to pieces before her eyes. She would never see her family, or Earth, or perhaps even another human again.

"Don't leave me here, Sam," she begged, not caring if the aliens heard her. "Please!"

Eighty-three million five hundred thousand, eighty-three million six hundred thousand...the lights on the booth to her right flashed green one last time, and the bidding stopped at eighty-three million six hundred and fifty thousand.

"SOLD!"

The next few minutes passed in a blur. Jane collapsed to her knees, and the guards carried her out to a holding pen, their sharp clawed fingers digging into her skin. Sam didn't come for her. No one came.

Alone, she fell to the stony floor and curled up in a ball.

As traumatic as the slave auction had been, the uncertainty afterward was even worse. Jane recomposed herself as best as she could, but the slavers were nowhere to be seen. She had no idea when they'd come back for her, and until they did, all she could do was wait.

"Now would be a very good time for you to show up, Sam," she said aloud in English. As humiliating as it would be for him to see her like this, at least she'd be free.

But it was becoming increasingly clear to her that Sam wasn't going to come.

At length, she heard the clacking of clawed foot-steps on the stone floor. Her arms tensed, and her heart pounded—it could only be the slavers. Sure enough, a squad of four guards rounded the corner. She took a deep breath as they unlocked the holding pen's door.

"May I ask who—"

"Silence!" said the chief guard, slapping her on the cheek.

That's eighty-four million credits you're slapping around, buddy, she wanted to snap at him. Instead, she held her tongue.

The guards led her down a long hall into a circular room. The stone floor gave way to sand, the blue-white sun shining through a pair of barred skylights in the vaulted ceiling. They marched her to the center and unshackled her chains.

"Stay here!" the chief guard ordered. Together, the slavers backed away from her, brandishing their shock prods as they did so.

Before Jane could ask what was going on, a conduit of shimmering blue light enveloped her. Her stomach fall and her heart leap into her throat as the room around her disappeared.

A teleporter.

When the blue light faded, she glanced around to get a sense of her new surroundings. The floor was made of polished marble and ebony, arranged in an artful checkerboard pattern. The walls were decorated with crimson velvet, with a luxurious divan full of pillows off to the side and a magnificent chandelier overhead.

Her heart sank. So she'd been sold into a kinky alien harem after all.

But then she noticed the foot locker next to the divan. It looked a lot like hers. Curious, she stepped forward. It *was* her foot locker—and her clothes were laid out on top of it, washed and neatly pressed.

Without a moment's hesitation, she snatched them up and hurriedly dressed herself. A surge of relief swept over her at the comforting sensation of her own clothes. Next, she opened her foot locker and did a quick inventory. To her surprise, everything was there, including all her work with the Setarni.

How were they able to get all of this? she wondered. Considering how much she had sold for at the slave auction, it had to have cost a staggering amount. What kind of aliens had that kind of money?

"Hello?" she called out. There was no reply.

Once again, the uncertainty began to gnaw at her. She made a more careful examination of her surroundings, unsure what to make of any of this. There were two doors, one of which led to a hallway, the other to a bathroom that was surprisingly human in design. Shower, toilet, sink, bidet—the only real difference was in the materials, which appeared to be some sort of plastic. But everything was perfectly functional, exactly like a bathroom back home on Earth. There was even a bar of soap next to the faucet.

She considered taking a quick shower, but decided against it. Instead, she washed her hands and face. That was refreshing enough.

Returning to the main room, she found that someone had placed a small table in the center, with a bowl of assorted baked goods and an opaque white beverage, not unlike a glass of milk. The discovery startled her: she'd only been in the bathroom for a few minutes, and hadn't heard a thing while she was there. Who were these aliens who had bought her, and why were they taking such pains not to show themselves?

Still, she had to admit that she was hungry. She cautiously picked over the baked goods, not sure if they were safe to eat, but when she finally tried one she found it quite delicious. Encouraged, she tried another. The beverage was sadly disappointing, with a sickly-sweet taste reminiscent of powdered milk, but the cookies were fantastic.

As she ate, the door to the hallway slid open. A tall, lithe Setarni stepped in, his blue facial tentacles hanging down in a sign of respect. He stopped inside the doorway and bowed.

"Greetings," he said—in English.

Jane immediately did a double take. "Hello?" she asked, unsure if she'd only imagined what she'd just heard.

"Allow me to introduce myself," the Setarni said, in standard colonial Earthspace English. "My name is Ivosh. It is my pleasure to be your host. How may I make you more comfortable?"

As a linguist, Jane immediately recognized Ivosh's hesitating speech patterns as a sign that he hadn't fully mastered the language. At the same time, he had no discernible accent, not even for a Setarni. Indeed, several of his words were morphologically impossible for a Setarni to produce, and yet he pronounced them as perfectly as another human.

But even that wasn't as shocking as what he'd just told her.

"My host?" she asked. "Aren't I supposed to be your slave?"

Ivosh's tentacles curled inward in a look of puzzlement. "If you would prefer a master-slave relationship, I can certainly—"

"No," she said quickly. "What I mean is I'm confused."

"An entirely understandable reaction," said Ivosh. "By now, you have no doubt recognized that I am not Setarni either."

"I wasn't going to ask, but now that you mention it..."

"Please feel free to ask me anything."

Jane blinked. She had so many questions, it was hard to know which one to ask first.

"Just to be clear, am I still a slave or aren't I?"

Ivosh twitched. "We are willing to release you, though the details of that arrangement would have to be negotiated."

"And my things?"

"They are yours, of course."

Jane sighed, letting out a breath she didn't know that she'd been holding. "That's very generous of you. But—why?"

"Why what?"

"Why pay so much for me, only to offer me freedom?"

Ivosh's tentacles wriggled in a gesture of amusement. "We prefer to think of you as an investment. Keeping you as a slave would not generate the returns that we seek."

So you do still want something from me, Jane thought to herself. Which was perfectly reasonable, of course. If they had bought her in order to free her— and from all indications, that seemed to be the case— then she owed them a great debt.

"Where did you learn English?" she asked, moving on to other topics.

"From the Hyadeans, your neighbors," Ivosh answered. "We are intensely interested in all things human. Your race is so new to galactic society. There is so much opportunity for mutual exchange."

"If you're not Setarni, then what are you really?"

"I believe the proper word would be 'shapeshifter.' Except, that is imperfect as well. The physical form is not nearly so important to us as the emotional."

Jane frowned. "What are you trying to say?"

"As a physical being, you require sustenance." He motioned to the plate of baked goods. "We, too, require sustenance, but not of a physical nature. Instead, we feed on—"

"Emotions?"

"Yes, that is adequate."

A chill ran down Jane's spine. "You feed on my emotions like a vampire?"

"It is not what you think!" Ivosh said quickly. His arms began to shake, and his facial tentacles turned white. "Please, do not be... distraught."

"What's wrong?"

"Please," Ivosh begged. "I assure you, our intentions are not... predatory. We have no desire to harm you."

"But you said you guys feed on—"

"You misunderstood. We do not... consume emotions the way a predator consumes its... prey, but as... a tree consumes... the light of your homeworld's sun."

He seemed on the verge of collapse. Jane took him by the arm and lowered him gently onto the divan.

"Just to be clear then, there aren't any negative side effects of this, uh, feeding?"

"None whatsoever, I can assure you."

"It doesn't take anything from me?"

"Not at all. Your comfort and pleasure is entirely our own."

It still didn't make much sense to her, but as she calmed down and accepted Ivosh's explanation, she noticed a marked improvement in his appearance.

"You're not just shapeshifters," she realized. "You're empath shapeshifters."

"That is correct."

"Whenever I'm upset, that hurts you. And whenever I'm pleased or happy, that gives you energy."

"Precisely."

By now, Ivosh had fully recovered. He rose to his feet, his facial tentacles a healthy blue.

"We are also merchants, but not in the traditional sense. We do not sell wares, but we do provide services."

"Services?"

"Yes. Our clients seek pleasure. We provide it for them."

Jane frowned. "Like a brothel?"

"Imperfect, but adequate. Not all of our services are sexual in nature."

And how many of them are?

Ivosh twitched. "Is something wrong?"

"No," Jane said quickly. "What do you want with me?"

"Nothing that would make you squeamish," Ivosh reassured her. "We simply desire someone knowledgeable who can teach us about your human culture. The opportunities for profitable intercourse with your species are truly immense."

"Profitable intercourse?

"You human emotions are more powerful than you know. Even now, you blaze like a sun. It is most intoxicating."

Jane wasn't sure how to take that. But then she realized what this was: a first contact opportunity.

Wasn't this what she had always dreamed of? To serve as an unofficial ambassador of Earth, and help to establish friendly and peaceful relations with the rest of the galaxy?

"I would love to teach you all I can about my species," she said. "It would be my pleasure."

"Excellent!" said Ivosh, his facial tentacles wriggling with delight. "But before we start, may I ask a small favor?"

"Certainly."

"Will you help me take a proper human form?"

Jane gave him a puzzled look. "I'm not sure I—"

"It will only take a moment. Please do not be alarmed."

His tentacles began to retract, and his skin began to change color. The joints in his arms and legs moved upward, and he grew a couple of extra fingers. In just a few seconds, the tentacles were replaced with a mouth and nose, and his skin color had changed to Caucasian white. As the details on his body took shape, a layer of skin peeled off to form dark pants and a turtleneck sweater. The process was a little grotesque, but thoroughly fascinating to watch.

"There," he said. "What do you think?"

Jane cringed. She didn't know how to explain it, but something was definitely off. Perhaps it was the eyes?

"You, ah, look a little—"

"Hold on. How's this?"

He transformed ever so slightly, improving from his previous form, but still a little off in the face.

"Not quite. Maybe if—"

"Then how about this?"

They went back and forth a couple more times. By the end, he looked a little like David Bowie: thin face, high cheekbones, and wild red hair.

"That's good," she said.

Ivosh smiled. "Imperfect, but adequate?"

"More than adequate."

"Excellent. Would you like me to take you to the captain now?"

"Wait—you're not the one in charge here?"

"Of course not," said Ivosh, chuckling in a carefully practiced manner. "Though 'in charge,' is not quite correct. We empath-shapeshifters travel together as a band, but each is free to come and go."

Like space gypsies, Jane thought to herself. *And I'm the first xenologist to establish human contact with them.*

"I would love to meet your captain."

"It would be my pleasure, miss…"

"Jane. Jane Carter."

From the opulence of her room, Jane expected the rest of the starship to be wide and luxurious. Instead, the hallways and antechambers on each deck formed a veritable maze. It was yet another reminder of how alien the empath shapeshifters were.

As she soon discovered, however, that didn't mean they couldn't look human if they wanted too.

"Hello!" said a young woman as they passed in the hallway.

"Isilibt," said Ivosh, kissing her on the cheek. "Allow me to introduce our new guest, Jane Carter of Earthspace."

Isilibt smiled and kissed Jane on the cheek as well. "Pleased to meet you, Jane."

For an instant, Jane thought she was looking at herself in a mirror. But then Isilibt's hair changed from blond to black, and her features smoothed out as if they'd been photoshopped. Just a few seconds later, and she looked like a girl from a pinup calendar.

"It's, ah, good to meet you as well," said Jane.

"I'm sure we'll see each other again. Don't be a stranger!"

Isilibt gave her a quick hug. Not sure how to respond, Jane stood a little awkwardly after she left.

"My apologies," said Ivosh. "Was our interaction unpleasant?"

"No," Jane said quickly. "It's just—I'm not used to that kind of intimacy with strangers."

"Oh dear. Have we made a mistake in our greeting etiquette? According to the Hyadeans, it seems to be a standard human custom."

"It's perfectly fine, just a little more European than I'm used to."

"European?"

"Never mind," said Jane. "I'll explain it later."

They passed a few others in the hallway, all of whom stopped just long enough to greet her and transform. Jane didn't know how they did it, but from gaging her reactions alone, they were each able to take on a unique human persona.

At length, they reached the bridge. It was surprisingly spacious, with a wide forward window that wrapped almost two hundred and seventy degrees around the room. Numerous chairs and control stations ringed the edge, while the captain's chair sat in the center. A slender young man rose from it to greet them.

"Jane, this is Captain Isiatuk. Captain, allow me to introduce Jane Carter."

"The pleasure is mine," said Isiatuk, smiling as he shook Jane's hand. His features were a bit elfish, like something from Lord of the Rings. While his presence was commanding, his manners were gentle and friendly enough that he immediately put her at ease.

"Thank you for, ah, purchasing me," she said.

"Of course. And I assure you, we have no desire to keep you as a slave. For all intents and purposes, you may consider yourself free."

"That's... very kind."

Isiatuk cocked his head in a close approximation of a look of puzzlement. "Does this arrangement fail to satisfy you?"

"It just doesn't make any sense. Why spend so much money just to free me? I get that you want to start taking human clients, but eighty-four million credits?"

"We have very... what is the human idiom?"

"Deep pockets," Ivosh offered.

"Yes," said Isiatuk. "We have very deep pockets. And of course, we do expect you to stay on with us for a while."

Jane nodded. "Definitely. I'm a xenologist, so I would love the opportunity to study your species."

"Then it appears that we've come to a mutually beneficial arrangement."

"But—why buy me?"

Isiatuk smiled and put a hand on her shoulder, dismissing Ivosh with a glance and a nod. He led her off to the side, out of earshot from the others on the bridge.

"I admit, when we arrived at the auction, I did not expect to raise our bid so high. But when we saw how your clashing emotions blazed with more energy than all of the rest of the audience put together, I knew that we could spare no cost."

"Was it really that powerful?"

"Yes. Even here from orbit, some of us reported that they could sense you. And if that is the case with all humans, the empathic energy at your homeworlds must be truly enormous."

"I suppose so," said Jane.

"I am curious, though. Who is he?"

"Who?"

"The man you were longing for."

Jane blushed. "I wouldn't put it like that. He's nobody. I was just a wreck."

"Nobody?" said Isiatuk, pointedly raising his eyebrows.

"Yeah. I mean, we both knew each other back at Sol, and he was with us on the convoy before the slavers came, but he's kind of a jerk. If I never see him again, it's just as well."

Isiatuk stared at her for a few moments before nodding. "Very well. In any case, welcome to the *Silver Diadem,* miss Jane. Do you have any other questions?"

"Yes. How long before we arrive in Earthspace?"

Isiatuk paused. "Unfortunately, the auction has strained our resources considerably. We will need to spend a few months replenishing them, most likely at the Gorinal star cluster."

"The Gorinal Cluster?"

"Yes. There are a variety of alien colonies there, with many opportunities for profit. But I assure you, our stay there will not be longer than a few of your standard Earth months."

"It's perfectly fine," said Jane. "I'm in no hurry."

"Very well. If there is anything we can do to make your stay with us a more pleasant one, please do not hesitate to let us know."

"Of course. And again, thank you."

They shook hands. Isiatuk returned to his command chair, while Jane lingered at the window. Outside, the blue-white sun began to rise over the dead, gray surface of the slaver world. It was a sight that Jane was sure she wouldn't miss.

Did she really mean all that about Sam? She had to admit, a part of her wondered if he was down there. But that was probably just because he was the only other human she'd seen in the last six months.

So long, Sam, she thought silently to herself. *You had your chance, and you blew it.* Thank goodness she didn't have to worry about running into that guy again.

Time and Space in Amish Country

It was early in the morning, somewhere between Toledo and Waterloo. I was sitting in the café car of the Capitol Limited, passing the time because I couldn't sleep. It wasn't just the shaking of the train, or the fact that the seats could never quite recline enough to be comfortable. I've slept on the train before, and I know all the tricks for getting a good night's rest. No, I couldn't sleep because I had graduated from university almost a year ago and still couldn't get a job. It was the summer of 2010, and the country was still reeling from the Great Recession. The only way I'd made it through the winter was by handing out fliers and distributing phone books from the back of my beat-up 1993 Honda Civic.

Most of my friends had moved back in with their parents, but I couldn't do that, and not just because it would be an admission of failure. My girlfriend was in Chicago and I knew our relationship would end if I moved back to Maryland. We'd been dating for the past three years, and if it weren't for the recession I probably would have married her, but money issues have a way of putting your long-term plans on hold. Our relationship was starting to feel like it had passed the expiration point: that we'd missed a crucial point of decision, and if we stayed on our current course we'd slowly drift away. Sticking it out in Chicago was the only way to extend the status-quo for a few more months, until I finally got my lucky break. But increasingly, it looked like that wasn't going to happen.

That nerve-wracking anxiety about the future, combined with the uncomfortable jolting of the train, made it impossible to get any rest. I sat in the café car with my head buried in my arms, drifting in and out of consciousness while waiting for the sun to rise and put me out of my misery.

That was when I saw him. He was a tall, gaunt-faced Amish man with a black wide-brim hat and a thick chin beard. Like all the other Amish on the train, he wore a clean blue shirt with suspenders and black pants. His little round spectacles were perched on the end of his bony nose, and he was reading intently from a newspaper that he held at arm's length away from him.

What would Sarah think of this guy? I wondered, thinking of my girlfriend. She had grown up Amish herself, but had left them during Rumspringa, the rite of passage when Amish teenagers are encouraged to explore the outside world and decide for themselves whether to follow the Amish way of life. Sarah had decided to give it up, and even though we didn't talk about it much, I could tell that she sometimes missed that world in the hills of Pennsylvania.

It was thinking about Sarah that made me notice the unusual headline on the paper that the Amish man was reading. It had something to do with an assassination attempt against the President.

Then I saw the name "Andrew Jackson."

Isn't that the guy on the twenty dollar bill? I thought, raising my head. *What's he doing in the newspaper?*

Soon, I began to notice other things. Instead of the usual cheap gray recycled stuff, this newspaper was printed on paper that was almost white. There were no illustrations on the front page, and the fonts were like something from a Spaghetti Western. And there was certainly no shortage of headlines. They sprawled artfully across the page in every font size from point 16 to point 48.

The Amish man glanced at me out of the corner of his eye and started. Without a word, he folded up the newspaper as quickly as he could and stuffed it under his arm. Then, he rose to his feet and left the café car.

"Wait," I said, raising my hand, but by then it was too late. The clacking of the tracks drowned out my voice as the door between cars slid open, and the man slipped through without so much as a backward glance.

Sarah didn't get off work until late. She waitressed at a small Chicago diner, just off the beltway.

With rent as high as it was, she worked all week and barely made enough to get by. When tips were good, she had enough for gas and groceries. When they weren't, her pantry would get frighteningly bare.

I used the cash my parents had given me to buy her some groceries. The door to her apartment was unlocked, which meant that her roommate was in. I didn't expect to see her, though: she played a lot of World of Warcraft and mostly kept to herself.

The exposed pipes that ran along the plaster ceiling were wet with condensation, and mold was starting to form again on the walls. I set the groceries on the table and sat down.

"Oh, hi there, Dan," said Sarah, walking in from the bathroom. "I didn't know you were in yet."

I'd texted her before coming, but she never checked her phone. It was an older Nokia model, the kind that's only useful for texts or calls.

"Hi Sarah," I said, rising to my feet. My hands slipped around her waist as I gave her a kiss. She gave me a quick peck, but let me go to pick up the cooking apron hanging from a nail in the kitchen wall. Disappointed, I sat back down.

"It was nice of you to buy groceries," she said as she started the electric stove. "How was your trip?"

"Long," I answered. "Couldn't sleep."

"You do look tired. Want to lay down on the couch?"

"Nah, that's all right."

The apartment couch had saggy springs and smelled funny. Sarah and her roommate had picked it out at Goodwill for twenty bucks. Even with the bed sheet they'd draped over it, I had no desire to go near it.

"I saw an Amish man on the train," I said. "It made me think of you."

"Oh?"

"Yeah. He was reading an odd-looking newspaper."

She set the cast iron skillet on the stove top and froze. For several seconds, she just stared straight ahead at the cracked paint on the wall. I frowned.

"You all right?"

"Yeah," she said, snapping out of it.

I stood up and walked over to her, putting a hand on her shoulder. "Are you sure?"

"Gotta put those groceries away," she said, hurrying to the table.

"What's wrong?"

"Nothing," she said quickly as she opened the fridge. "I just think it's funny that an Amish man made you think of me."

"Well, you did grow up Amish, didn't you?"

She said nothing.

"There was something else," I said, giving her a hand with some of the dry goods. "The newspaper he was reading said something about Andrew Jackson."

"Andrew who?"

"You know, Andrew Jackson? The guy on the twenty dollar bill?"

"Oh, him."

"Anyway," I continued, "the newspaper said something about an assassination."

Her eyes widened. "Was he killed?"

I looked at her funny, not sure what to make of her reaction. It seemed that she was genuinely surprised about something that had happened more than a century ago. Even if she wasn't too sharp on her US history, it didn't make sense that she would be so upset by it.

"Sarah," I said, looking her in the eye. "What's going on?"

She bit her lip and tried to put the rest of the groceries away, but I put my hands on her shoulders and stopped her.

"I don't know what you want me to say, Dan," she said, folding her arms. "Everything's fine, except..."

"Except what?"

She sighed heavily. "Except the stuff that isn't. I mean, look at this place. The mold, the mice, the fact that I work all day and can barely afford groceries— and you're not doing much better. How's the job search?"

"Shitty," I admitted. "Is that what's bothering you?"

"I don't know, Daniel. Not anymore."

She pulled away and finished putting away the groceries as I watched. I got the distinct feeling that she was slipping away—that we were both slipping away from each other, and there wasn't anything I could do to stop it. The quiet panic left the taste of vomit in my mouth.

"I wish things could be different," I told her. "I mean..." My voice trailed off.

"We've been over this," she said. "When you can afford a better place, we'll decide what that means for the two of us. Until then, it doesn't make sense to make any long-term plans."

"Dammit!" I shouted, punching the cinderblock wall. My sudden outburst made her jump. Pain shot like lightning through my knuckles, but I didn't care.

"Dan!"

My throat constricted, and I fought back by taking a deep breath. Even so, I couldn't keep from shaking. Sarah ran to my side and put a hand on my arm.

"It's okay," she said softly. "We'll get through this. Things will get better."

"Will they, though?" I asked. "Everyone says that we're in a 'jobless recovery' now, but if anyone's recovering, it certainly isn't us."

"Don't give up. You'll find something."

"And what if I don't? How long are you going to wait for me, Sarah? It isn't fair of me to drag you through this, this—I don't even know. And you know what the worst part is?"

"No," she said softly. Her eyes started to tear up.

"It's that I don't even know who I am any more. The crap jobs, the never-ending job search—it's like I'm drowning, Sarah. Growing up, everyone told me to pursue my dreams, but after college that just doesn't seem like an option anymore. Another year, and if nothing changes, I don't know what will become of me. Or of us."

For a long time, neither of us said anything. My bloodied knuckles stung like crazy, but at least it gave me some relief from the overwhelming numbness.

"You want a change?" Sarah asked.

"Yes. Don't you?"

She nodded slowly, as if unsure whether to continue.

"What is it?" I asked.

"I know how we can get away from all of this. It won't be easy, though. It might not even be a good idea."

"What have we got to lose?"

She mulled that over for a moment, then nodded. "Have you paid rent yet?"

"No."

"Good. Pack your things and use the rent money to buy a bus ticket."

"But what about my security deposit?"

"Forget about it," she said. "If this works out, you won't be needing it."

I frowned. "Why? Where are we going?"

"Amish country."

I can't tell you how liberating it felt to just walk out of my shitty apartment, never to see it or the city of Chicago again. Even if things didn't work out, I doubted either of us were ever coming back.

In Lancaster, we walked around for a couple of hours until Sarah found the people she was looking for. It was almost as if they were expecting us. Soon, we were in a horse-drawn buggy driven by a thirty-something Amish man named Obadiah. The concrete and asphalt of the city gave way to blue sky, rolling hills and wide, green fields. The air was fresh, and the good clean smell of earth seemed to permeate everything.

"Before we arrive, there's something I should tell you," Sarah said. The buggy jostled us a little, but we hadn't yet left the paved road.

"What is it?"

She swallowed and glanced out the window before answering. "I'm not actually Amish."

I laughed. "What are you talking about?"

"I mean it, Daniel. That whole story about leaving the Amish community for Rumspringa was just a cover. I would have told you earlier, but there wasn't any way to do it until now."

"That's ridiculous. How else did you get us here?"

"You wouldn't believe me if I told you."

Her words made me stop laughing. I put a hand on her knee.

"Don't say that, Sarah. Of course I'd believe you."

"Would you?" she asked. Her eyes pleaded for me to believe her, even though the rest of her seemed to doubt that I would.

"Yes," I said simply.

"Promise?"

"Sure."

"All right," she said, taking a deep breath. "I'm a time traveler."

I didn't know what to say, or how to even respond. Several long, awkward moments passed, during which the clatter of the horse hooves and the bouncing of the wheels were the only things that broke the silence. Sarah's expression fell as I struggled to come up with a response.

"That's, uh... that's interesting."

"It's not just me. Most of the Amish are time travelers, too. They're guarding a natural time portal deep in the hills of Pennsylvania. I found out about it in 1830 and sneaked past them to come to your time."

Sweat began to form on the back of my neck. I couldn't help but think of the security deposit I'd left behind in Chicago. That was $300 I was never getting back.

"Daniel?"

"Oh yeah, right. Time portal."

Sarah's expression fell. She could tell I wasn't buying her story.

"You don't believe me."

"No, Sarah, it's not that at all. It's just... well, I was expecting to try out the Amish life for a while, and if you're saying that's not—"

"Don't lie, Daniel. You don't believe me."

I didn't know what to say to that, so I did the worst possible thing and said nothing.

"It's all right," she said, her expression turning to stone. "Obadiah can give you a ride back to Lancaster, where you can get a ticket back to your parents' house. I'm sorry."

"And what about you?"

"I'll be fine."

We said nothing for the rest of the buggy ride.

There's something about Amish country that clears the mind. In the city, where you're surrounded on all sides by concrete, glass, and steel, there's a tendency to never look up from the ground. In that sense, it's not all that different from a prison. In Amish country, though, you can't help but sense the vastness of the world all around you. Who would have ever thought that getting closer to the Earth actually helps you to look up from it?

For most of that buggy ride after our conversation, I felt sick to my stomach. The quiet panic converged on me, and with it all of my anxieties about the future. But by the time we reached the end of the line, I'd come to a decision.

Obadiah pulled the buggy up to an old farmstead, piles of hay scattered evenly across the adjoining field. An old-growth forest lay on the opposite side of the unpaved road.

"This is as far as you go, English," Obadiah told me. "Sarah, best come along with—"

"No," I told him. "I'm staying with her."

He turned around in his seat and frowned, his beard pulling up in disapproval. "What was that?"

"I believe you, Sarah," I said, turning to her. "I want to come with you."

"Are you sure?"

She looked at me with eyes full of hope. It had been a long time since I'd seen that in her eyes before. It made me want to put my arms around her.

"We've come this far, haven't we? I don't know anything about a time portal, but if it's good enough for you, it's good enough for me."

"Daniel..."

Obadiah muttered something in Pennsylvania Dutch and left us for the farmhouse. The horse's ears twitched as he swatted at flies with his tail.

"He's probably getting one of the elders," Sarah explained. "The members of this settlement are the ones responsible for guarding the time portal. I'm pretty sure they'll let me through, but I don't know about you."

"I think I can convince them."

An old man with a snow-white beard and a crisp straw hat followed Obadiah over to us. He walked with a bit of a stoop, though his arms were as strong and his hands were as calloused as Obadiah's.

"Greetings, English. What brings ye to these parts?"

"Do you recognize me?" Sarah asked.

The old man squinted and jutted his chin out at her. "Sarah Foster, is it? I heard you were coming back. Who is this with ye?"

"My name is Daniel, sir," I told him.

"Well met, Daniel. What kind of a seeker are ye? The English don't come to these parts idly."

"I'm with Sarah. We've come seeking the time portal."

For several moments, the old man just stared at us. In the window of the farmhouse behind him, I could see half a dozen Amish children staring at us as well. Doubts crept into my heart as I realized just how ridiculous my request had sounded, but the old Amish elder didn't laugh.

"I'm afraid I can't let ye come with her, English. Ye don't belong in these parts, and she doesn't belong in yers."

"You're wrong," I said, taking her hand. "We belong together. Sarah, will you marry me?"

"What?"

I got down on one knee, looking up at her wide, startled eyes.

"I don't have a ring, but I hope you'll forgive me for that. We've let too much come between us as it is. This is something I should have done a long time ago, the recession be damned."

"What are you saying, Daniel?"

"I'm asking you to marry me, Sarah. We can figure out the details later."

She frowned. "Are you sure?"

A lump rose in my throat as the words came of their own accord.

"All this time, I've thought of marriage as a sort of crowning moment—an ending, if you will. That's why we put it off for so long, in the face of so much uncertainty. But I see now that it's a beginning, not an ending. And if I have to face an uncertain future, there's no one else I'd rather face it with."

For a single heart-rending moment, Sarah was silent. Her hands were trembling, but the rest of her was deathly still. She took a deep breath, and a smile slowly crept across her face.

"I thought you'd never ask."

"Is that a yes?"

She pulled me to my feet and gave me the tightest hug of my life.

"'Twill be better to marry ye on the other side," the Amish elder told us. "If that is what ye desire. But ye cannot cross alone. If either of ye want to cross back, ye'll have to cross back together."

"You really believe me about the time portal?" Sarah asked. "You don't think I'm crazy?"

"Not any crazier than me at this point."

She gave me a cockeyed smile. "You'll like it on the other side. The country's still young and full of opportunity. It will take a lot of hard work to make it, but at least in the nineteenth century we still can."

"It sounds perfect."

"Are you sure you don't think I'm crazy? That's the Amish's main way of guarding this place, you know. They don't need to use force if no one from the outside world would believe us. And since the Amish keep to themselves, no one ever—"

I silenced her apprehensions with a kiss. She melted into my arms, and I knew it was enough.

A Hill On Which To Die

Is this the hill on which you want to die?

The sky was a perfect cloudless blue, the high mountain air thick with the scent of pines. Garak-Nur took a deep breath, refreshing his body and clearing his mind. Around him, the other members of the orcish war party waited eagerly for the duel that would decide their leader. His challenger Alak-Dar stood ready to receive him.

"Are you going to fight me, you old goblin? Or have you grown too senile to draw a blade?"

Garak-Nur grinned as he drew his trusted sword, Blacknife. There was a time long ago when he had taunted his war chief, just as this upstart now taunted him. It was good for the young to challenge their elders—it ensured that the strongest and bravest would always lead them. For most of Garak's life, that had been him, but now his leathery skin was sagging, and his once-proud tusks were dull with age and wear. His left knee ached from a wound that had never fully healed, and the scars that criss-crossed his chest were too old to inspire fear.

I'm an old, grizzled veteran who's lived more than thirty-five years, he thought to himself. *Alak-Dar is young and mighty, much as I was at his age. The clan would fare well under his leadership. Yes, this is a good place to die.*

"What was that, you toddling little runt?" Garak shouted back. "Did your mother give you a knife with which to play? I've eaten man-children larger than you—come at me, and we'll see if your flesh is as soft as theirs!"

Alak-Dar's nostrils flared, and he bared his tusks in a show of rage. "You should never have left the burrows, you rock-headed fool!" With a sudden high-pitched battle cry, he lifted his sword and charged.

His opening blow was a powerful one, but Garak deflected it with skill belying his age. Alak's sword swept back to parry a murderous riposte that Garak sent slicing at his throat. He made a feint, but Garak did not fall for it. Instead, Garak sidestepped and renewed the attack, giving his opponent no quarter.

The blades sang loudly in the high mountain air, ringing in the ears of the entranced orcish warriors. The fight was evenly matched—neither of the duelists had the upper hand.

"You fight like a half-blind she-orc," Alak taunted. "Is your strength flagging like your fat belly?"

Garak was too wise to let his temper get the best of him. However, Alak was right—his strength was slowly ebbing. If the fight drew on much longer, he was apt to lose by attrition.

Realizing this, he leaped back and tossed Blacknife from his right hand to his left. Alak, sensing a trap, hesitated just a hair's breadth before lunging forward. In that moment, Garak read his opponent like a map. He sidestepped easily and rammed Blacknife into Alak's groin, slicing up through his stomach and spilling his hot, black entrails onto the ground. Alak-Dar fell to his knees, disbelief written in his wide, yellow eyes. With a furious scream, Garak pulled Blacknife free and swung it in a mighty arc, sending his opponent's head rolling down the hill like a stone.

"Does another wish to challenge me?" he shouted. His voice echoed from the heights of the snow-capped peaks, but the rest of the war party was silent.

Garak called his war-dog and mounted the beast in one swift motion. With Blacknife held high over his head, the ebony blood of his vanquished opponent dripping down his wrist and arm, he turned to his orcish warriors.

"Then let us stain our swords red with the blood of the man-children!"

At this, the warriors drew their weapons and let loose with a mighty war cry. The mountain air rang with the shrillness of their fury and the ardor of their unquenchable blood lust. Garak-Nur drank it in like a fiery balm, reveling in the privilege that was his to lead them.

Not this hill, he told himself. *Not today.* He threw back his head and screamed at the cloudless blue sky.

* * * * *

The moans of pleasure resounded through the dark, twisting halls of the clan burrows. In the great hall, the victorious warriors fell with lusty passion on the she-orcs who waited to receive them. They had fought well and looted much, and through the rowdy orgy that now met Garak's ears, their strength would be passed to a new generation of orclings.

Garak sat by the entrance to the armory and thought on the raid that he had led. The man-children had been caught by surprise, and the resulting slaughter had been glorious. The few armed woodsmen had been forced back into the tavern, which a volley of incendiary arrows had set on fire, burning them all alive. Garak's warriors had slit the throats of their women and children and gorged on their frothing blood. A few had been taken captive to sell to the slavers; they now huddled whimpering in a cavern off of the main hall.

Only a dozen or so of Garak's warriors had been slain, all of them barely more than orclings. This had been their first raid, and they'd thrown themselves stupidly on the enemy's flank without noticing the woodsmen hidden in the trees. But Ilika-Zan, Garak's second-in-command, had led the counterattack that had resulted in the burning of the tavern. While Garak's warriors had looted and burned the settlement, Ilika had gathered the man-children's flocks and led them into the mountains. Because of him, the clan would feast on mutton for many months to come.

"Good raid," said Ilika, rounding the bend with his sword slung over his shoulder. A hardy veteran like Garak, his muscles were sinewy but firm, his tusks yellow but sharp. His gray skin was still speckled like an orcling, though his hair was long and his chest hoary. His breastplate hung loose from the straps around his neck—even in the burrows, Ilika preferred to wear his armor.

Garak grunted and nodded. "Indeed it was. We'll have to take another war party out soon, though. Too many damn fool runtlings who don't know the point of a sword from the pommel."

"We'll weed them out," Ilika agreed. "Harden the others, turn them into a firm fighting force. When Braknar's horde comes over the mountain again, we'll be ready for them."

Braknar was the leader of Lone Peak, a rival clan from the northern end of the mountain range. They were mortal enemies of Garak's clan, the Great Crag, and had been at war with them for countless generations. Five lesser orc-clans vied for territory in the foothills, but the mountains belonged to Garak and Braknar.

A high-pitched squeal down the hallway gave way to a panting moan. Garak chuckled.

"Why aren't you in there with the rest of them?" he asked Ilika. "I expect a warrior of your stature to sire no less than a dozen orclings tonight."

"Oh, I'll join the fray soon enough."

"Getting old, eh? You should take a harem—you'd have your pick of the clan. Hell knows you've earned it."

"Soon enough," Ilika muttered. "Speaking of harems, why aren't you with yours?"

Garak groaned and rose wearily to his feet. "I suppose I should see to them. Even an old-timer like me has a duty to his clan."

"If I ever consider it a duty and not a pleasure, may the Dark Lord himself rise from the grave and sever my leathery head."

The two orcs laughed uproariously. Garak was glad that he could jest with Ilika. Many in the clan wondered why Ilika hadn't challenged Garak for command—Garak himself sometimes wondered. But Ilika was content to be Garak's right hand, and a stronger, more loyal warrior he'd never seen.

Garak mused on this as he crept down the dark and winding hallways toward his harem. The shrill and ecstatic peals of the younger generation grew fainter the deeper he went, until they were little more than a rumbling above his head.

"There you are," came a sultry orcish voice as clawed hands pressed him up against the wall. "I've been waiting for you."

"Nili," he muttered, his voice turning to a lusty growl as her tusks nuzzled his chest. Nili was the first concubine that he had ever taken. Others had come and gone, but like a gnarly wind-tossed bristlecone atop an arid, craggy peak, she had stayed with him throughout it all. No other orcish concubine had shown as much loyalty to her harem-chief as she had shown to him.

At twenty-eight, Nili was nearing the end of her childbearing years, and her hair was streaked with silver just as Garak's. Even so, they clawed each other's backs and nipped each other as playfully as orcling youth. The din of the orgy in the great hall made Garak painfully aware of his age, but in Nili's arms, that hardly mattered.

He lay with her afterwards for some time as his vitality slowly returned. They said nothing, but the way she caressed his chest told him that she was content. If she hungered for another coupling, she was careful to hide it. They both knew that he would have to conserve his strength if it was to last the night.

Bira was the next concubine in Garak's harem. She said not a word as Garak entered her chamber, but received him as dutifully as a war-wolf receiving a rider. Garak had acquired her in a raid on one of the lesser orc clans in the foothills, and while she never offered any resistance to his advances, coupling with her was like coupling with a dead fish. There was no pleasure as he strained to perform his duty, all the while taunted by the youthful cries from the orgy above.

Exhausted and slightly repulsed, he left her chamber almost as soon as his duty was done. But that proved to be a mistake, for his youngest concubine was waiting just outside.

"There you are," said Enid, her lips etched with a scowl of envy. "Took you long enough."

Few she-orcs were as lithe and supple as Enid. Her skin was as smooth as suede, her hair as soft as corn-silk. Her tusks were as pale as milk, and her claws as sharp as knives. Many a warrior had gazed upon her lustily, wondering why such a nubile young she-orc would bind herself to a single partner when she could have her fill of all the warriors in the clan. Yet Enid carried a secret, the shame of which condemned her to seek refuge in an old orc's harem. While all the other she-orcs replenished the clan with strong and healthy orclings, Enid was as barren as sulfurous slag.

Nevertheless, her body burned with the same hunger as the orcs in the great hall above. And so, as Garak took her in his arms, she seized on him with a passion that was as strong and as furious as raw blood lust. He strained as hard as he could to satisfy her, but her youthful hunger demanded more than he could give. Passion gave way to desperation, desperation to frustration, and frustration to rage and fury. It was a pattern they repeated often—a pattern he knew all too well.

"You always come to me worn out and exhausted," Enid murmured, her claws speckled black with his blood. "Why do you never save any of your strength for me?"

"I'm... trying," Garak moaned, but his excuses were pathetic, and he hated himself for making them.

"Why do you come to me last, after you've given your best to all the others? Why can't you come to me first for a change?"

Because it would be an insult to Nili and Bira, he thought silently. Every harem had a rank and a pecking order, and to overlook that order for the convenience of one concubine would only sow discord. Besides, if he went to Enid first, he wouldn't have any strength left for the others.

Enid rose up off of him, a look of disgust on her face. "I don't know why I put up with you," she said. "What do you think I am, some kind of trophy? Is that why you keep me, you old goblin?"

"Would you rather I released you?" Garak-Nur growled.

"Ilika-Zan isn't nearly as impotent as you," she went on, ignoring him. "I heard he can pleasure more than a dozen she-orcs in one night. If I were his concubine, I wouldn't be so barren."

Garak bared his teeth and snarled. If Blacknife had been by his side, he would have gutted her. Instead, he swallowed his rage and rose to his feet.

"That's enough," he said, putting on his loincloth. "We're finished here."

"You were finished before you even came to me."

Garak swiped at her with his claws, but she easily sidestepped the blow. Growling angrily to himself, he stormed out of the chamber before she could hurl another insult. She was right, of course—his vitality had ebbed much in his old age. But if he released her from his harem, it would bring shame to them both. Was Enid so blind that she couldn't see that?

No matter, he thought grudgingly as he entered the torch-lit hallway. He of all orcs knew better than to fight on a hill where victory would gain him nothing.

"Chief Garak-Nur, a messenger from the Northlands has arrived."

Garak downed his mutton with the last of his tankard of beer. Around him in the Great Hall, the other orcs looked up with interest at the news.

"Messenger? What sort of messenger?"

"A human messenger, chief," said the young warrior. "And a mage by the looks of it, too. We tried to kill him, but he fried Soso and Arec to a crisp and demanded to see you."

Garak grunted and wiped his mouth. A human mage from the Northlands? He'd heard rumors from the slavers about a rogue sorcerer trying to establish a stronghold up there. The slavers had said he was buying slaves by the hundreds—more than they could possibly supply. Perhaps the messenger was from him.

"Send him in," said Garak. "And assemble all the warriors in the great hall. We'll show this arrogant man-child that his magic is no match for our might."

A cheer rose up in the great hall as the warriors ran for the armory. Those who already carried their swords ushered the orclings and the she-orcs down to the nesting chambers, where they would be safe. The preparations were swift and thorough—Garak smiled to his commands carried out with such vigor.

"It would not be wise to slay this messenger," Ilika whispered as the warriors readied their swords. "We already have enough enemies in the Northlands."

"Do not worry," Garak assured him. "If he is who he claims to be, I fully intend to let him live. But first, let us impress upon him the greatness of our strength, so that his master will know to respect us."

"Of course. I stand ready at your command."

When the mage entered the cavern, a great war cry met his arrival. The walls and ceiling trembled with the sound of more than a thousand orcish warriors, their swords gleaming in the torchlight. But if the display of strength impressed the arrogant man-child, he refused to show it. His expression was impassive, his eyes hid beneath the peaked hood of a woolen cloak. A traveler's scrip hung from one shoulder, with a small purse of coins dangling from his belt. He carried no weapon except a small hunting dagger sheathed by his hip and a knobby staff with a black onyx gemstone set at the top. The onyx glimmered, and not just from the light of the torches.

Garak raised a fist, and the warriors gradually grew silent. He rose from his seat at the head of the hall and narrowed his eyes.

"Who are you, man-child, and what brings you to our burrows? Speak!"

"Greetings, oh great chief of Great Crag," said the messenger, bowing without approaching him. "I am Zvabeg, servant of Algaroth, mighty Witch-King of the North." He spoke with a voice loud enough that every orc in the great hall could hear him clearly.

"What do the orcs of Great Crag have to do with this Witch-King? Why should we care about the affairs of your master?"

"It is said that the orcs of old were created to serve the Dark Lord," Zvabeg answered. "When the Dark Lord's soul was cast into the formless void, the orcs were scattered across the face of the earth. But now, a new Dark Lord has risen in Algaroth. He invites the orcs of Great Crag to join with him and restore the ancient glory of your race!"

"Do you take us for fools?" Ilika-Zan bellowed. "Why should we share our glory with those of the lesser clans? No clan is as strong or as dauntless as Great Crag!"

The warriors in the hall took up the thunderous war cry, once again making the caverns quake. But Zvabeg, with his eyes still hidden under the hood, only grinned.

"Well spoken, great warrior. Why indeed should you bow to the level of your inferiors? No orcs of any clan are as strong, nor as swift, nor as cunning as those I see before me now."

At Zvabeg's words, the hall grew silent. Instead of looking to their chief, the warriors looked to the man-child, their curiosity piqued by his flattery.

"The Witch-King is building an army of orcish warriors. They will need many war chiefs to lead them—chiefs and chiefs-of-chiefs, generals with thousands under their command. Who better to lead them than the mighty orcs of Great Crag?"

Garak frowned, while next to him, Ilika narrowed his eyes. What game was this man-child playing?

"We have no desire to serve this Algaroth," Garak shouted, his voice booming throughout the chamber. "We are free orcs who pay tribute to no one. Our only allegiance is to ourselves."

"But why should you content yourselves with the meager plunder of this mountain wilderness when the entire world lies before your grasp? The armies of Algaroth will sweep across the land, striking fear into the hearts of kings and emperors. One day, he will subjugate every race beneath his rule, and those who fight under his banner will all share in the spoils."

"How many war chiefs?" one of the warriors shouted. Garak bared his teeth, but he could not recall the question.

"If every warrior of Great Crag became a chief, there would still not be enough to lead the Witch-King's armies," said Zvabeg. For the orcs gathered in the hall, that was enough.

"And what of the rest of the clan?" Ilika bellowed, but Garak knew that they had already lost. The eyes of the younger warriors gleamed with the prospect of power and glory, of rising higher and faster than they ever could beneath Garak-Nur. Zvabeg's flattery had fanned their greed and ambition into a raging inferno, and there was nothing Garak or Ilika could do to stop it.

"Lone Peak has already pledged itself to the Witch-King," Zvabeg said, his lips curling in the barest hint of a smile. "But I am certain that the orcs of Great Crag would lead the armies better."

All at once, the hall erupted into a tumult of excitement.

"He's right! We could all be war chiefs!"

"How would you like to lead a thousand warriors?"

"Let the elders look after the clan! I'm for joining the Witch-King."

Ilika-Zan growled and rose angrily to his feet, his teeth bared and his hand on the hilt of his sword, but Garak stopped him.

"Careful, Ilika. We must tread carefully."

"But this is intolerable! How can we stand by while this silver-tongued man-child entices the whole clan with his empty promises?"

Is this the hill on which you want to die? Garak asked himself. If he refused to join forces with the Witch-King, he risked inciting a riot, in which he and Ilika would be killed and his successor would join the Witch-King anyway. It was one thing if the matter could be settled by a duel, where all would respect the outcome. But this—this was subversion. Never before had his authority as clan chief hung by a thinner thread.

"We will consider your offer," Garak told Zvabeg, eliciting a triumphant grin from the man-child. "Now go, and return in a fortnight."

"Very well, Garak-Nur. But be careful not to let this opportunity slip through your claws. I will return in half that time—farewell."

The looks of naked disappointment on his warriors' faces made his heart sink. Had he led the clan for so long, only to be undone by the flattering lies of a man-child? But the damage was already dealt, and there was nothing he could do to erase it.

"Ilika-Zan," he said softly as the great hall rumbled with restless excitement.

"Yes, Garak?"

"Assemble a war party in secret of those whose loyalty you do not question. Have them gather arms and provisions for a long march, and if any of them have harems, have them bring their concubines as well. Gather them swiftly—we leave tonight."

Ilika frowned. "What do you have in mind?"

An exodus, Garak thought. But to Ilika, he gave no intimation of his plans.

"All will be clear soon enough. Now go!"

"As you command, Garak," said Ilika. He pressed his fist to his chest and left the great hall.

"Where are you taking us?" Enid complained loudly as she and the other concubines followed Garak down the hall. "I don't see what's so urgent that you call us out of—"

"Silence!" Garak hissed. "Speak again and I'll slit your throat!"

The warning was unusually harsh, but it had to be. With most of the clan fast asleep, they had to move as stealthily as possible. If anyone discovered what they were doing, it would be certain death for all of them.

As Garak led them warily past a cluster of sleeping orcs, Nili walked up close beside him.

"What are you planning?" she whispered.

"If I tell you, will you still follow me?"

"You old fool," she said, taking his clawed hand in hers. "When have I ever left your side?"

He glanced over his shoulder before leaning close to answer. "Most of the young warriors of the clan yearn to join the Witch-King. If I were to refuse, they would rise up against me and join with him anyway. Therefore, I am taking my loyal followers away to form a new clan."

"A new clan?"

"Yes. But speak of this to no one. If word gets out—"

"My lips are sealed."

Garak smiled. He knew that he could trust Nili to keep her word. If it pained her to leave any of her offspring behind, she made no sign of it.

They hurried through the cool, dark caverns, occasionally stepping over an orc who slept drunkenly in their path. Garak yearned to call his war-dog—the beast would serve them well in the coming march—but she was sleeping with all the other dogs and pups in the main chamber, and calling her would only alert the others. They would have to make the journey on foot.

The crescent moon hung low in the sky when they stepped outside, the milky white band of the galaxy glowing bright in cool night. Garak took a deep breath, filling his lungs with the crisp autumn air.

"*Now* can you tell us what's going on?" Enid asked, her voice petulant.

Garak answered her with his blade. It rang loudly as he drew it from its sheath, shattering the stillness of the night. He pointed it at her, and the disdain in her eyes gave way to terror.

"Silence!" he hissed. "On pain of death, do not speak until dawn. Understand?"

Enid dared not protest. Garak sheathed his sword.

"Now follow me," he growled.

They found Ilika-Zan and the rest of the war party a short distance down the mountain. Six orcish warriors were trussed up like chickens—no doubt they had been on watch to guard the burrows when the party had secretly assembled.

"Garak," said Ilika, thumping his chest in salute. "What are your orders?"

Garak surveyed his orcs. Many of them were too young to have harems, and those few who did had concubines who were growing old. The she-orcs had managed to bring only half a dozen war-dogs, most of them pups and too young to ride. The concubines and warriors looked to him in confusion, unsure of his plans. Nevertheless, there was trust in their eyes—trust born of the victories he'd never failed to give them.

"Have you secured the provisions?"

"We have," Ilika answered. "Enough for a three-month journey."

Winter will be here before then, Garak realized. *Foraging will be hard in the coming months.*

"I will explain everything at dawn," he told his warriors. "Until then, know only that our lives depend on marching as far and as fast as possible. We cannot afford to let any drop out, lest our flight be discovered. Ilika will keep to the rear and slay any stragglers."

"What of the prisoners, chief?" one of the warriors asked.

Garak peered down at them. Some of them had fear in their eyes, while others looked up to him in confusion. Clearly, none of them had expected their own chief to treat them in such a way.

Should we kill them? Garak wondered. He could ill afford to carry prisoners, and if they returned to the burrows they would surely wake the others. But to kill them? Until just a few hours ago, these orcs had been his, bound to him by clan and by blood. If he killed them now, without any obvious cause, the loyalty of the others might waver.

"String them up from the great pine at the mouth of the ravine," Garak ordered. "That is, unless any of them want to join us."

He eyed them one by one, his gaze as sharp as a scythe. Four of them averted their gaze, but the last two stared at him with the same look of trust that he'd seen in the warriors Ilika had gathered.

"Will you join us?" he asked softly. "You will never be able to return if you do."

They hesitated, but nodded. Garak made a gesture, and one of his warriors stepped forward to cut them free.

"Make haste with the others," he ordered. "We leave within the hour."

"Which way?" Ilika asked.

Garak thought of the Witch-King in the north, seducing his mighty warriors with empty dreams and false promises. A vast wilderness valley lay to the south, but it was the surest way to put the Witch-King behind them.

"We go south," he grunted. "Let's move."

They marched hard through the night, staying close to the ridge line as they descended into the foothills. The concubines kept pace for the first half of the march, some of them even pulling out ahead, but soon they grew tired and began to fall behind. Without mature war-dogs, they all had to march alike, even those who were used to riding. Thankfully, Garak's warriors marched with cold, iron discipline, and the she-orcs other than Enid made no complaint.

"Is it wise to march so swiftly through enemy territory?" Asta-Van asked as they scouted ahead. "If this were a raid, I'm sure we could take them, but we have our concubines to protect."

Asta-Van was a seasoned veteran who had drawn swords with Garak-Nur since before many of the others had been born. One of his offspring, Narad-Yur, marched with Ilika in the rear. Although Asta-Van was old for an orc, he had brought with him a harem of four young nubiles, the most of anyone.

"The foothill clans will not attack us if we're out of their territory by daybreak. They'll be too confused to pursue us effectively, and wary of an attack on their rear."

"Good point," Asta grunted. "We will quicken our pace."

"No," said Garak. "The concubines are straggling. It is not good to stretch ourselves thin in enemy territory."

"You quicken the pace and leave the stragglers to us," said Nili. In the darkness, Garak hadn't noticed her come up. "Bira and I will keep them marching, even if we don't stop until noonday!"

Her words made Garak smile. There was a fire in her eyes that seemed almost to light the darkness.

"Very well, but let them know that Ilika-Zan will slay all who straggle just as surely as will the warriors."

"Of course," said Nili. She turned and disappeared into the night.

"Tough one," Asta remarked. Garak grunted, and the march went on.

They reached the wilderness just as the sun broke over the valley to the east. The light was blinding, the air dry and cloudless, so the orcs were happy to reach the shade of the trees. The scouts killed two deer, and the warriors dug hungrily into the fresh meat, bloodying their faces and claws.

"How many stragglers?" Garak asked Ilika as the war party assembled among the nearby boulders.

"None," said Ilika, "though some of the younger concubines almost didn't make it. We need to keep as many of them alive as we can, though, right?"

Garak nodded. An unspoken understanding passed between them that this was no war party, but an exodus. Surely the others must have guessed it by now, but it was time to lay the rumors to rest. When the warriors and concubines had eaten their fill and the deer carcasses were little more than clean-picked bones, Garak stepped forward.

"My warriors," he said in a loud voice. "Last night, I told you I would explain the purpose of our march at first daylight. By now, I am sure you have realized that this is no ordinary war party."

He surveyed the gathering, his gaze passing from face to face. All eyes were on him, and every ear listened intently. Garak-Nur chose his words carefully, knowing that his fate as their leader was poised on the edge of a knife.

"You are here because I trust you not to fall for the smooth-tongued flattery of the Witch-King," he continued. "His messenger may have seduced the others with his empty promises, but you know just as well as I do that to join forces with him would spell disaster for our clan. But since the others will not see that, I have brought you out from them, so that we can start a new clan across the wilderness."

"A new clan?" Asta said aloud. The others frowned, and a rumble of hastily muttered conversations rippled through the assembly.

"Yes," said Garak. "A new clan, free of the Witch-King or anyone else who would enslave and dominate us. We will live and die as free orcs!"

"Here? In the wilderness?"

"Does this mean that we'll never go home?"

"What about the she-orcs and the orclings? Will we never see them again?"

"If we start a new clan, they'll kill us if we go back!"

Garak drew his sword Blacknife, the blade ringing in the still morning air. *Is this the hill on which you want to die?* he asked himself. If he was to die here, he would do so with his sword in hand.

"Are there any who wish to challenge me?" he bellowed, silencing them. "If so, let them step forward!"

"They will have to challenge me as well," said Ilika-Zan, drawing his sword and standing beside him. "I didn't march all the way out here only to crawl back on my belly, begging for mercy!"

An awful silence fell across the gathering. None of the younger orcs would dare to challenge two battle-hardened veterans, but Garak could see the shock of betrayal etched on their faces. In time, that shock would give way to anger and resentment, which would tear them apart unless it was given an outlet. But here in the wilderness, there were few settlements to raid, and their numbers were too small to justify losing even one warrior.

"You sniveling little runtlings!" Nili shouted, joining Garak and Ilika at the head of the assembly. "Do you miss the soft breasts of your mothers? Even if you could go back, the Witch-King would lead you off with his armies and you'd die on some distant battlefield, without a she-orc to mourn you. Can't you see what Garak-Nur has done? He's given you a chance to win all the glory that Zvabeg promised you, and more. When we establish our new clan across the wilderness, the tales of your exodus will be the legends that mothers teach their orclings by the firelight."

One of the warriors raised his voice. "But how were we supposed to know—"

"You weren't," Nili answered. "Garak-Nur chose you for your loyalty—he knew that he could trust you to follow him into the gaping jaws of hell itself. If that's true, then what is to stop you from following him to glory and a new home?"

"Gods bless that she-orc," Ilika muttered. "She's like the mother we all wish we'd had."

"She'll be a mother to this clan before the exodus is done," Garak agreed. He sheathed his sword and stepped forward.

"Hear me, my warriors," he said in a loud, commanding voice. "We will build a new home even greater than the first. Our burrows will run deep and our territory will spread wide. We will raid the homes of the man-children with swords of fine steel, and drink their blood like new wine. Every warrior will have a harem with as many concubines as he can satisfy, for while the other clans join the Witch-King, we will raid their burrows and carry off their she-orcs by the dozen!"

His warriors let out a cheer—a weak one, but a cheer nonetheless. Nili's words had softened them, but Garak's words now steeled them to face their fate with their blades drawn and their heads held high.

Not all the orcs accepted Garak's words. Enid stewed for almost an hour before she brought herself to confront him.

"How could you do this to us?" she screamed, scratching wildly at Garak's chest. "Take us back to Great Crag—take us back, now!"

Garak grabbed her by the wrists and tried to throw her off, but she would not be thwarted so easily. She hissed and bit his hand, making him let go, then slashed his face with her claws. The blow made him wince, and when he wiped his face with the back of his hand, it came away smeared with thick, black blood.

"How could you betray us all like that? Why didn't you tell us what the hell you were planning to do? And what is your plan? Where are you taking us? Into some wilderness, where we'll all be slaughtered by woodsmen or dwarves? You're worse than the orcs of Lone Peak—at least if they'd kidnapped me, I'd have a safe burrow in which to live."

"Silence!" Garak-Nur roared. His hand reached for Blacknife, but Ilika stepped between them before they could fall on each other.

"This squabbling is useless," he said, looking from Garak to Enid. "Garak-Nur has decided for us, and we cannot return to Great Crag. Let us look to the future instead of dwelling on the past."

Half of the orcs in the war party now looked on the dispute with curiosity and interest. Garak scowled—he knew that Enid's rage echoed the fears and misgivings of many of them. What Nili had worked so hard to build, Enid was carelessly tearing apart. Couldn't the damn she-orc see that? Couldn't she see that she was undermining their whole future?

"And Garak," said Ilika, lowering his voice to keep the others from overhearing. "I know you're angry, but we can't afford to lose even one she-orc—not if we're going to start a new clan."

If only you knew of Enid's barrenness, Garak thought bitterly. Still, Ilika was right—this fighting was pointless.

"Well spoken, Ilika," he said, drawing himself to full height with as much dignity as he could muster. "But I do not need your help to manage my own harem."

"Damn right you don't!" said Nili. She took Enid by the ear and twisted until she squealed. "You stupid orcling brat—who do you think you are to treat our harem-chief like that? One more outburst from you, and I'll claw your face a sight worse than you clawed his!"

Gods bless you, Nili. He could have embraced her right there, but with his warriors watching, he watched impassively as the older concubine dragged the younger one off.

"How's your face, chief?" Ilika asked. "Should we stitch it?"

"Stitch it? Ha! I rather think it suits me. It certainly matches my other wounds, don't you think?"

The warriors in earshot chuckled at Garak's brazen contempt at the offer of help. The cuts on Garak's face still stung, but he knew that his orcs would take heart from his show of strength. They needed to know that their leader would not be bowed by pain. Garak was more than a war chief to them now: he was an anchor of stability, an ancient and immovable mountain in the face of a coming storm. At the slightest sign of weakness, everything would come crashing down.

A scout rode up on a war dog. As he pulled up his mount to hard stop, the scout's eyes gleamed with excitement.

"We found a band of man-children!" he reported, loudly enough that the others could hear him. "A pioneer wagon train!"

"Where?" asked Garak.

"In the wilderness, not five miles distant. They've got about twenty women and children, and only a dozen grown men between them."

"What sort of guard to they have? What weapons do they carry?"

"Not much, chief. Bows and arrows, some daggers, maybe a sword or two. Nothing we can't handle. They're trying to move quickly, but their wagons are having a hard time making it through the forest. Why, the trees are so thick, we came up close enough to spook their oxen and the man-children didn't even see us!"

"It's the perfect chance for a raid," said Ilika, his sharp teeth gleaming as a smile spread across his face. "What do you say, Garak? Shall we draw swords?"

"I think we shall," said Garak. He drew Blacknife and turned to his warriors. "Who will join me to gorge on the flesh of man-children?"

The answering cry was resounding. The orcish warriors, still struggling with the news of the exodus, seized upon the raid as an outlet for their pent-up frustration and rage. It was exactly what Garak needed to mold them. Once they had tasted of blood and victory, they would no longer see themselves as the warriors of Great Crag, but as the fathers of a new clan.

The raid was a success. The human settlers were indeed as undefended as the scout had claimed, and Garak's warriors made quick work of them. The orcs only suffered three casualties: two young warriors, both barely more than orclings, and Asta-Van.

The grizzled old veteran threw himself in front of an arrow that had clearly been meant for Garak-Nur. Few had noticed his act of sacrifice, and the battle soon became too frenzied to mind the loss. But Garak was so astounded that he hung back while the others surged forward.

"That arrow was meant for me," he told Asta, who lay dying at his feet. Black blood trickled around the edges of his mouth, staining his age-worn tusks.

"No," said Asta-Van. "You must... lead the others... find a new home. It is better... for me to die."

"You will not be forgotten, friend," Garak said softly. Asta's lips turned up in a smile, and his spirit passed into the void.

With no one to claim his harem, Asta's four young concubines fell to the rest of the clan. The warriors, aroused by the taste of blood and the thrill of killing, took to the mourning she-orcs with all the lust of an orgy. It soon became apparent that four young concubines were not enough to satisfy the frenzied warriors, and soon they were screaming in pain and terror.

"That's enough!" Ilika shouted, pulling the warriors away amid snarls and protests. One of Asta's former concubines lay naked on the ground, unmoving as if she were dead.

"We can't afford to lose any of them," he told Garak later. "The she-orcs, I mean. It takes more than warriors to start a new clan."

He was right. The few old veterans with harems didn't have enough concubines to replenish the clan with new orclings. Besides, Garak saw deep resentment in the faces of those warriors who had no concubines. It would be very difficult to keep morale high when there were no orgies for them to look forward to after each successful raid. They would have to acquire she-orcs as soon as possible.

But that was only one of many pressing matters. Winter was coming, and with it, the threat of starvation and cold. They were camped in an open wilderness with no caves and few natural obstacles to shield them. They desperately needed a new home—a place to dig new burrows and root themselves to the stony earth.

In the hour before sunset, when the rest of the clan was fast asleep, he finally had the chance to tend to his harem and rest his old, hoary head. Enid refused to talk to him and Nili was content to let him rest, but Bira came softly to him before he fell asleep.

"We're no longer with Great Crag?" she asked.

Garak-Nur nodded with a grunt.

"Great Crag is an enemy to us now? We're not of their clan, and never will be again?"

She spoke of Great Crag with such contempt that he sat up and stared at her in surprise. Ever since the raid in which he'd carried her off captive, she'd never shown so much as a hint of emotion. But now, it seemed as if the dam holding back the grief of all those years was finally beginning to break.

"That's right," Garak told her. "We're free-orcs now—Great Crag is behind us forever."

She took a deep breath and stared off at the old mountains, her tired old eyes yearning for something unknowable. Then she turned to him and pressed a hand on his chest.

"Never again," she whispered, more to herself than to him. Garak was too tired to come up with an answer, but that hardly mattered, because she nuzzled up to him with a passion that made words seem trivial and awkward. While the others slept, they coupled in a way that they never had before. As they coupled, it seemed that a piece of Bira's newfound vitality passed from her to Garak. For a few brief moments as he held her in his arms, he forgot the weariness of his many years, and when he finally slept, she slept contentedly beside him.

The clan awoke a few hours after nightfall, and under Ilika's leadership they broke camp and prepared for another long march. They had a long distance to travel, crossing the wilderness valley to the mountains on the other side. No one knew what they'd find there, but they knew it would offer more safety than the wilderness valley. Even if death waited for them on those wild and rocky slopes, they pressed on to meet their fate.

On the third night's march, the party reached the foothills. The scouts reported no sign of rival orc clans, but Garak knew better than to believe that the territory was unclaimed. He had his warriors march with their swords drawn, and kept the main body as close to natural defensive barriers as possible.

On the fifth night, the scouts reported abandoned mine shafts, most likely of dwarvish origin. Garak ordered an immediate halt—dwarves were deadlier than orcs, and if there were dwarves in these mountains, it might be best to skirt around them in search of another range. The younger warriors itched for a fight, but Garak knew that they were in no shape to launch an invasion. Without any burrows to fall back to, and with no way to replenish their losses, he could ill afford to lose any of his warriors. Stealth, not strength, was the key to their survival now.

The next night, he went up with the scouts to the mines. After a little exploring, they found a stone gate leading straight into the mountain. The doors were made of polished granite and stood almost three times taller than Garak. They were inscribed with runes and carvings, but the edges were cracked and broken, and one of them stood off at an angle on broken hinges. Whoever had once lived there, it was clear that they had left some time ago.

"Let's go in," Garak ordered. They tied their war dogs to a black pine by the entrance and stepped through the dwarvish gate.

They entered a cloistered hall, with high vaulted ceilings and beautifully carved statues lining the walls on either side. The statues seemed eerie, like dwarvish warriors turned to stone to guard the entranceway. Their cold, stony eyes seemed to watch Garak's every move.

One of the warriors swung his club and smashed the head off the nearest statue. It hit the floor with a crash and broke a score of mosaic floor tiles. Garak hissed and drew his sword.

"Do you want to get us killed?"

"N-no, chief," said the warrior, Blacknife pressed up against his chest. His eyes were wide with terror.

"Then don't announce our position like that."

"Sorry, chief."

They walked past the cloistered hall and down a magnificent stone staircase. It opened up below them to a short row of barracks, weapon racks in the center with armor stands against the walls. Except for two rusted axes, the racks were empty.

The next level opened up to long rows of workshops and forges extending out from the central stairwell. Ashes lay scattered across the floor, with wrought iron tools sitting on stone work benches and leather aprons molding on hooks against the wall. At some of the workshops, there were still unfinished crafts sitting where their creators had abandoned them.

By now it was clear that this was no mine, but an abandoned dwarven stronghold.

"Go to Ilika," he told the youngest of the orcs in the scouting party. "Tell him to bring the clan into the hallway above us and to set guards by the stairwell to wait for our arrival."

"Yes, chief."

He clasped the warrior's shoulder and looked him in the eye. "Under no circumstance is anyone to follow us down here. They can take shelter in the first level, but must come no further."

"But chief, the dwarves are all gone."

"Yes, and what about the thing that drove them out of here?"

The warrior's eyes widened.

"Right, chief. I'll get the message to Ilika right away."

He scampered up the stairs with speed born of terror. *That's one less coward to make a mess of things,* Garak thought bitterly. He turned to the others and saw varying degrees of fear in their eyes. How many of them would run in the face of danger? He could ill afford any more cowards now.

They continued their descent through the abandoned stronghold. On the third level, they found a magnificent feasting hall, almost twice as large as the great hall in their old burrows. The tables were cracked and broken, the wooden chairs half-burned. Great black scorch marks criss-crossed the walls, and piles of blackened armor sat amid splintered bones.

So this was where the battle was, Garak mused as he led the scouting party onward. *But who makes war with fire underground?* There were only a few possibilities, none of which bode well.

Downward they descended, past dormitories, personal quarters, stockpiles, and a spacious mausoleum. In the center of the mausoleum, they found a magnificent tomb with a gold-plated sarcophagus encrusted with ruby and onyx. Runes proclaimed the dwarf chief's history and accomplishments, but none of the orcs could read it.

"Break off the gold plating," Garak ordered, "but only enough to carry in your hands. Leave the rest to salvage later."

The scouts complied, making quick work of the beautifully crafted tomb. Unlike the dwarves, they had no lust for treasures or precious metals, and did not hesitate to reduce the sarcophagus to scraps of broken gold. If they grumbled, it was because the treasure would make it difficult to draw their swords.

The air in the lower levels of the stronghold was fetid with sulfur and brimstone. The stench grew stronger the further they descended, until it was almost unbearable. The scouts covered their mouths with bits of torn cloth, but Garak made no sign of discomfort. Now, of all times, his warriors needed him to be strong.

Is this the cave in which you want to die? he asked himself. He would have preferred a hill, with hundreds of his orcish clansmen to witness his glorious demise. But if danger lurked in these old, abandoned halls, it was better to face it by himself than to lead his whole clan unwittingly into the jaws of death.

They reached the bottom of the staircase and stepped through a crevice into a natural cave. A flickering red light illuminated the stalactites and stalagmites from behind, making them glow in the darkness. From the far end of the cave, Garak heard the sound of a great beast breathing.

"A dragon," he muttered, pulling out his knapsack. He dumped the contents onto the ground. "Here—give me your gold and treasure."

"But chief, what if—"

"I'll go talk with him alone. Stay back, and if the dragon kills me, return and warn the others."

The orcish scouts nodded and complied without further protest. The gold from the tombstone filled Garak's knapsack almost to overflowing, but he grunted and hefted it over his shoulders. As an offering to the dragon, it would do quite nicely. Blacknife was useless against such a beast, but he kept it if only to die with it in his hands. Any other death would be shameful.

He rounded the bend in the cave and came within sight of the dragon. It was an enormous serpentine beast, with dark scaly skin and claws as long as Garak's forearms. Its wings were narrow and spindly, its legs short but powerful, and its tail ended with sharp, bony spikes that were long enough to impale a troll. Its snout was pointed and narrow, nuzzled up against its tail, and when it exhaled, tendrils of flame shot out between its teeth, casting flickering light across the cavern.

The dragon sat on a modest pile of treasure, no doubt taken from the dwarves. Rubies, emeralds, sapphire, and diamonds; silver goblets and glazed marble statues; rings, bracelets, and anklets all made from the finest gold were only a few of the many riches that filled the beast's horde. Garak sneered—the legendary greed of the dwarves was eternal, but here, it had only sealed their doom.

"Oh great lord of dragons!" he shouted. "Slayer of dwarves, destroyer of strongholds, dread beast of smoke and flame! Your servant trembles and bows before you!"

"Who disturbs my slumber?" said the dragon, its nostrils flaring with fire. Its catlike eyes flew open.

"I am Garak-Nur, orcish war chief and father of the—" here he hesitated, realizing that his clan didn't yet have a name. The pine trees overlooking the abandoned mine shafts came immediately to his mind, standing tall and free beneath the clear blue sky. He had always enjoyed the smell of pine, and now, deep in the bowels of the earth with the sulfurous stench of the dragon all but choking him, he longed for the open air and the cool mountain breeze.

"—the Black Pine Clan!"

"Orcs, eh?" said the dragon, stirring awake. "Nasty creatures, orcs. Far too greasy."

"I have brought you a tribute, great dragon lord," Garak bellowed. He lifted the knapsack high in the air and poured its shimmering contents onto the ground.

"Hmmm," said the dragon, purring as it considered the treasure. Compared to the rest of his horde, it was a meager offering indeed, but not so meager as to be insubstantial.

The dragon reared up with its fiery snout mounted menacingly at Garak. "You have my attention, orc. What do you want?"

"My clan has wandered far across the wilderness," Garak explained, trying very hard to ignore the searing heat of the dragon's breath. "We are searching for a new home, and desire to settle in the ruins above your lair."

The dragon sighed, its hot breath singing the hair on Garak's arms. "I suppose it was only a matter of time before someone tried to move in. You're not after my treasure, are you, orc?"

"Not at all, great dragon. We are orcs—we care not for such useless trinkets."

"Trinkets indeed," the dragon chuckled, smoke rising from the edges of its mouth. "The pest has no need for treasure of its host. Is that what you are, orc? A pest?"

Garak's hair bristled, but he bowed on one knee. "Not at all, great dragon. I swear on my life that we shall not disturb you."

"Indeed you should swear on your life, orc, for I could snuff it out with a single breath. Why, then, should I permit you to dwell above my lair?"

"We shall be your first line of defense. Any thief who wishes to plunder your horde will first have to fight a path through us—and I assure you, that will not be easy."

At this, the dragon purred. "Interesting—very interesting. But can you offer anything to sss-sweeten the deal?"

Flames hissed out of the dragon's mouth, making Garak sweat. He closed his eyes and waited for it to pass. Now, of all times, he had to remain firm. The dragon might torch him where he stood, but if he ran, his warriors would never follow him into battle again. The shame of his humiliation would spell his doom.

"We will conduct many raids in these parts," Garak answered, "and when we do, we shall offer you the treasure of our spoils." It was just as well—they had no use for gold and silver, and gemstones held as much interest for them as baubles.

"I would expect no less," said the dragon. "But the wealth of this wilderness is too sparse to grow my lair. I hunger not only for gold, but for sacrifices of flesh."

Garak winced as he considered how best to appease this demand. "Then we shall offer you the flesh of our fallen comrades, which—"

"Orc flesh? Ugh, how disgusting! What makes you think I want rancid orc flesh when I can barely stand your stench as it is?"

"Forgive me," said Garak, bowing to hide his relief. "What manner of flesh do you desire?"

The dragon smacked its lips. "Human flesh is quite succulent, and surprisingly difficult to obtain. If you wish to dig your burrows above my lair, you must offer me a sacrifice of human virgins—plump, and not too sinewy—each fortnight."

"It shall be as you demand, great dragon lord."

"That is not all," said the dragon. "You must also clean the dung from the cave I use as my refuse pit."

At that, Garak bristled. "Clean your refuse pit? What do you take us for, goblins?"

The dragon let loose a burst of flame which exploded against the wall an arm's breadth to his right. The heat melted his hair and singed his skin, silencing him immediately.

"It's my lair, orc, and if you'll live above it you'll do as I say. My refuse pit needs cleaning and you're just the ones to do it."

We'll have to enslave a colony of goblins to do the dirty work, Garak thought. *Dragon's dung is good for growing mushrooms, so the goblins will produce a surplus which will supplement our food stores.*

"As you demand, great dragon. We shall offer you human sacrifice and see that your refuse pit is cleaned."

"Very well, orc. We have a deal. But if you ever slack in your obligations, or if any of your orcs so much as touches my treasure, I shall exact a high price from you and your clan."

Garak-Nur drew Blacknife and sliced the palm of his hand. Making a fist, he let his blood drip onto the cavern floor.

"With this blood, I seal our allegiance and swear that clan Black Pine shall serve you so long as we dwell within these walls."

"Yes, yes, of course. Now leave before you make a mess of yourself. Disgusting creatures, orcs..."

As Garak returned to the crevice where his warriors waited for him, a grin crept across his old, weathered face. A dragon with no taste for orc-flesh, in a stronghold left for ruin—it was more than he had bargained for. And not only had his clan found a home, but they had found a name, too. Black Pine—it had a pleasant sound to it. The tall, dark pines that grew on the mountainside would soon become their watchword, and orclings that grew up beneath their shadow would come to associate them with home. They would fight to return to the cool, windy shade of the dark green boughs, and the last memory their minds recalled as they lay dying on the battlefield would be the scent of pines in the crisp mountain air. Yes, it was a fitting name—a fitting place to call home.

"You call this a burrow? It's more like a stinking trash heap!"

Enid tossed her hair disdainfully at the sight of the dwarvish ruins. Garak-Nur growled and clenched his fists, but resisted the urge to speak back. Enid was not so courteous.

"You kidnapped me from my home and marched me across a wilderness... for this? It's pathetic! The halls are too wide, the ceilings too tall, and the draft—why, I bet the whole stronghold is as drafty as this cavern. And look at all this rubble! You expect us to clear it out? It'll take months!"

"Then we'll just have to square our shoulders and get to work," said Nili. "You should be grateful that—"

"I'm not finished, you old hag! Unlike you, I'm not fool enough to be blinded by vain hopes and impossible dreams."

Hot blood rushed to Garak's face, and his fingers twitched uselessly. He could lead his warriors fearlessly into battle, face death without flinching, but managing the youngest concubine in his harem was too much. It was all he could do no to draw Blacknife from its sheath and cleave her in half.

The other orcs were starting to take notice, and a small crowd soon gathered around the cloistered entrance hall. The provisions and supplies were now safely stowed in the new burrows, and the warriors had nothing to keep them from this curious confrontation between their old war chief and his beautiful young concubine. Ilika walked up to them, clearly to give a progress report, but stood back aways as Enid unleashed her pent-up fury.

"You think we'll survive the winter here? With a fire-breathing dragon below us and miles upon miles of empty wilderness in every direction? And even if we do, where are you going to find she-orcs to replenish the clan? Even if we do survive the winter, we'll all be dead in another generation, and these ruins will be just as empty and abandoned as they were when you found them."

"You sniveling little brat!" Nili sneered. "Have you no pride? These burrows are your home now, and Black Pine is your clan. If you find this place unlivable, then perhaps you'd like it better out in the wilderness."

Enid laughed, the bitter sound ringing throughout the cloistered halls. "You think I'd like it better in the wilderness? Perhaps I would! If a war chief from one of the lesser clans carried me off right now, I wouldn't complain. You call these ruins a home? This trash heap isn't fit to live in, just as Garak-Nur isn't fit to lead a harem!"

"Foolish she-orc!" Garak bellowed, his rage exploding. "You find my harem unlivable? Well, then I release you! You are no longer my concubine—you are free."

Silence fell in the cavern like the silence following a thunderclap. The warriors who before had listened with idle curiosity now turned to the dispute with active interest. Enid's face fell, and her cheeks turned sallow.

"W-what do you mean?" she stammered. "Are you really—"

"I mean that we are divorced, you maleficent she-orc. You no longer have any place in my harem. You are free—free from my protection, free from my debt, and free to face the whims and mercies of the world alone."

"Does that mean that we can take her, chief?" one of the orcs shouted. The resentment among Garak's warriors had been growing, with some arguing that all of the concubines should be made common with the rest of the clan. From the way that his warriors looked on with glee, Garak knew exactly what would happen to Enid now that he had divorced her.

A pang of guilt stabbed at him, but it was deflected by his rage. "She is common with you all now," he answered. "Do with her as you will."

Enid screeched and ran, but Garak's warriors were faster. They caught her between the pillars and pinned her to the ground. She snarled and snapped, fighting back with all her strength, but the orcish warriors who pressed upon her were too strong to be deterred by violence. Their eyes gleamed with a deep, lustful hunger, and though Enid's claws drew blood from many of them, that only frenzied them all the more.

"Stop!" she screamed. "Stop!"

"Call them back," said Ilika, at once by Garak's side. "This cruelty is needless—the clan cannot afford to lose even one she-orc."

"She'll live," said Garak. "She's tough—she can handle them."

"Handle the whole clan? By all the demons in hell, Garak—she's your own damned concubine!"

"Not anymore," he growled.

Her screams were ragged now, her clothes in pieces all over the floor. She sounded less like the haughty, self-righteous concubine that Garak had come to resent and more like a terrified man-child. Garak's rage began to subside, giving way to shame and regret.

It was wrong for me to do this, he realized. *But there's nothing that I can do about it now.*

"At least give her as a gift to one of your warriors," Ilika pleaded. "She'd make a fine trophy—any of us would be honored."

"You know full well I can't do that, Ilika. There's already enough resentment against those of us who have harems—giving her as a trophy would only make that resentment grow."

"But to make her bear the whole clan all at once? It isn't right—not like this!"

"Then stop them," Garak said softly. "But wait for the frenzy to die down a bit first. I don't want them to turn on you—I can't afford to lose you."

Enid's screams turned to whimpers and gurgled pants. The first of the warriors began to leave the orgy, their faces scarred black with blood, but smiling all the same. The sight made Garak disgusted, at himself as much as the scene before him. He turned and led Nili down the dwarvish staircase without another word.

* * * * *

Enid survived, thanks to Ilika's intervention. She joined Asta-Van's former concubines, and Garak gave a strict command that there would be no more orgies until they had enough she-orcs to equal the number of their warriors. There was considerable grumbling at this, but the warriors accepted it without challenge. As for Enid, she never spoke with Garak again.

With the anger and resentment coming to a head, Garak-Nur left Ilika-Zan in command of the burrows and organized a war party for the purpose of acquiring she-orcs. Almost every warrior in the clan wanted to join, but Garak sent back almost a third of them, mostly the younger ones who had little skill in battle. This angered many of them, since they had hoped to start harems of their own. One of them even challenged Garak for command, but Garak made quick work of him, holding up the warrior's severed head as an example. That quenched their rage for a while, but he knew that it did little to quell their resentment.

He led the war party down from the mountain and into the foothills, but found no sign of any rival orc clans. He led them into the valley in the hopes of abducting females from a human settlement, but the only villages they found were fortified with earthworks and pickets, and every caravan was under heavy guard. Word of their previous raid must have spread among the man-children for them to be on such high alert.

With few other choices left to him, Garak took his war party north, toward the mountains of Lone Peak and Great Crag. His warriors took cheer as they drew closer to the territory that they knew so well. It was with great reluctance that Garak led them within sight of Great Crag, though, for he knew that the clan could ill afford deserters at such a precarious time.

They had barely entered the foothills when the scouts gave an unusual report. An orcish war party almost twice the size of theirs was traveling south toward the wilderness, but it was not a party of warriors —it was a party of she-orcs. They were dressed for battle and carried all manner of weapons, but that was where the similarities ended. There were even armed orclings marching among them.

The news spread through the war party like wildfire. She-orcs and orclings, taking up swords like warriors? It was unthinkable. Never before in all their history had she-orcs been known to fight. The scouts' reports sparked much discussion and many ribald jokes, but for Garak, it was no laughing matter.

That night, he called a war council among his veteran warriors to discuss their plans. They all agreed that the she-orcs would be a great asset to the clan, but none of them advocated taking them by force. If they won, it would be a Pyrrhic victory, and if they lost, it would be a disgrace. A few argued that the she-orcs might join them willingly, but the others argued against that, saying that it was unwise to assume that armed orcs from another clan, even she-orcs and orclings, would be willing to surrender.

In the end, they decided that the most prudent course of action was to head off the she-orc war party and see how they responded. They marched swiftly that night to a field before the pass to the wilderness. Lest the she-orcs take it for an ambush, they positioned themselves conspicuously in the open, just outside the trees.

The sun rose slowly around the ridge line of the nearby mountains, melting the autumn frost where the light met the edge of the shadows. Garak's warriors went nervously about their morning routines. They were used to raiding and didn't like to fight defensively.

A she-orc scout rode out on the far side of the meadow, took a long look at them, and rode back into the forest. The warriors silently put on their armor and prepared for the worst.

It took only an hour for the she-orc war party to gather on the far side of the meadow. They formed ranks quickly with weapons drawn, showing little discipline but little fear either. Garak's warriors marveled at the sight of so many she-orcs bearing swords. A tall, broad-shouldered she-orc dressed in the armor of a war chief stepped forward, a great curved sword in her hand.

"I am Nari-Sen of the clanless free-orcs you see before you," she said in a voice loud enough that all could hear her. "Who speaks for this war party?"

Garak stepped forward.

"I do," he answered in a voice just as loud. "I am Garak-Nur, war chief of Black Pine."

"Black Pine? Pah! I know you, Garak-Nur. You are the disgraced former war chief of Great Crag. Did the Witch-King's offer not suit you? Or did you abandon your clan out of cowardice?"

A murmur went up among Garak's astonished warriors. Garak himself growled, but swallowed his rising anger.

"It was not cowardice that drove us, she-orc, but the thirst for freedom. The Witch-King has enticed many with his empty lying promises, but we know that to join him is to become his slaves. We will never yield ourselves to become slaves to any man-child. We are the orcish warriors of Black Pine, and we are and will forever be free!"

His warriors shouted and cheered at his words, banging their swords on their bucklers and creating a noise that echoed throughout the hills. Nari's lips turned upward in a smile.

"Well spoken, Garak. Your thirst for freedom is one that we share. When the he-orc warriors of our clan left to join the Witch-King's army, an emissary came demanding 'volunteers' for the purpose of breeding. We rebelled and slew the he-orcs who would stop us. Now, like you, we wander these mountains seeking a place where we can be free."

"If that is true, Nari-Sen, then why should there be swords drawn between us? Join us, and we will welcome you freely into our clan."

"Never!" Nari screamed, lifting her sword high above her head. "We did not earn our freedom only to give ourselves up to your rag-tag band!"

At this, her she-orc warriors lifted their weapons and cheered. The sight was so unthinkable that Garak's warriors knew not how to respond. They looked to him as if expecting the command to fall on Nari's band, but did not seem eager to fulfill it.

Though the she-orc numbers were more than twice that of Garak's war party, however, he noticed that their shouts were no louder. In fact, there were some among them who weren't even cheering at all.

Perhaps we have an opportunity here, he thought. He remembered the flattering words of Zvabeg, and how the man-child had turned his own orcs against him.

"We do not ask you to be our slaves," he shouted, "but free orcs like ourselves. We live in a great abandoned stronghold built by dwarvish hands, on a mountain where no other orc-clan dwells. The air is crisp and the water clear. Our warriors are strong and will give you many fine orclings."

"Orclings? Pah! There is more to life than bearing orclings. We don't need you, he-orc!"

In spite of her vociferous cries, many of her warriors shifted uneasily, looking from side to side at each other. It was clear enough that not all of them shared Nari's sexless vision of freedom.

"Then what will you do, Nari-Sen?" he asked. "Will you fight us here? Force us to spill your blood? Or will you turn north to the lands of the Witch-King? No, Nari—join us, and let us be free together."

For several long moments, Nari stared at him in stony silence. The tension between the two opposing war parties was greater than that of a taught rope.

One wrong move by any of them, and the hillside would run black with blood. Garak fingered his sword, waiting for Nari's response.

Without warning, she threw her head back and laughed. The two war parties grew deathly silent at the sound. Her laughter echoed through the mountains, coming back like an unearthly cry.

"I see your game, Garak. Very well—if anyone's blood should be shed, then let it be yours alone."

Garak frowned. "What do you mean?"

"Since you are so set on having us join you, let us decide this dispute in true orcish fashion: by a duel to the death. If you win, you can take us to your burrows. But if you lose, you will let us pass freely!"

What is her game? Garak wondered. If, by some strange fate of luck, she managed to strike him down, then his enraged warriors would take up arms to avenge their disgrace. Surely Nari could see that. And how could she, a she-orc, hope to cross swords with a hardened veteran warrior and come away with her life? It seemed the height of folly.

Still, he drew Blacknife without protest. He'd heard enough of her hubris—better that she alone should die than drag all her followers with her.

"I accept, she-orc."

"Then come at me, you toothless old he-goblin! Show me what you've got!"

A grin spread across Garak's face to be taunted in such a way. For all Nari's hubris, he had to admit she was spirited. It was a pity she had to die, but blood-lust was stronger than pity.

He lifted Blacknife and charged with a ferocious battle cry. She easily dodged his attack, striking at his throat, but he deflected it without difficulty. He struck back with a murderous riposte, but she leaped out of reach of his blade and parried the following blow. What Nari lacked in strength, she more than made up for in speed and agility. Her technique was not as practiced as Garak's, but her valor was unparalleled.

They squared off, their eyes meeting across the small, deadly space. Garak saw no fear there—only cold, focused concentration. He tried to draw her out with a feint, but she read him correctly and sent a blow slashing across his face. He leaped back in time to escape it, but her blade still drew blood.

A collective gasp went up, though whether from Garak's warriors or Nari's, it was impossible to tell. Nari let loose a shrill cry and pressed her advantage. He saw an opportunity to riposte, but his attack was too slow and she sidestepped him easily. Her sword slashed up, and another gasp went up among the orcish warriors. Hot blood seeped from a wound across Garak's belly—a wound that stretched the breadth of his forearm. He clutched his hand to it and staggered back.

She could have gutted me with that, he thought, realizing that the slash was only skin deep. *She could have killed me.*

"Are you ready to die, you old he-goblin?" Nari asked, taunting him. "Shall I give you a moment to pray to your gods?"

"I haven't said a prayer in my life," Garak growled. He raised his sword in preparation to attack.

"Then perhaps now is a good time to start."

Nari's warriors began chanting, "Na-ri! Na-ri!" Their cries echoed off of the hills and mountains. In response, Garak's warriors took up their own chant: "Ga-rak! Ga-rak!" The chants and shouts grew louder until they rang in Garak's ears like a drumbeat pounding out his doom.

Is this the hill on which you want to die? he asked himself. Nari-Sen raised her sword, and the sight made him chuckle. Who's hubris was greater: hers or his? He saw that he'd grossly underestimated her, but there was no turning back now.

With a blood-curdling war cry, he hurled himself at her, swinging Blacknife in a death-dealing arc. Nari's eyes widened, and her parry failed to deflect the blow. She ducked at the last moment, and Garak's blade clipped off a tuft of her hair. An instant later, she made a parry that knocked Blacknife from Garak's hand. With the pommel of her sword, she struck him across the face and sent him spinning to the ground.

All the orcs on the hilltop grew silent—so silent that Garak could hear the mountain breeze. He lay on his back, staring up at the sky, and mused to himself how beautiful a sight it was. It made him feel free to lie beneath such a limitless blue expanse, and that feeling of freedom made him smile. He had fought a good fight, he had given all for his clan, and their future, though uncertain, would rest in competent hands. Yes, this hill was a good place to die.

But death did not come. Nari-Sen stood over him with her foot planted squarely on his chest and pressed the tip of her sword against his throat, but she did not strike.

"Lay still, you old goblin," she said softly. "You'll get your she-orcs." Then, turning to Garak's warriors, she bellowed in a voice loud enough that all could hear her.

"Behold your war chief, warriors of Black Pine! Does it surprise you to see him fall at my hand? Then know this, you runtlings—no sword that is lifted against Nari-Sen and her band of orcish she-warriors shall prosper!"

Garak could hear the snarling protests of his warriors, but without a chief to lead them, they would not charge the enemy on their own. From the triumphant grim on Nari's face, he saw that she knew this all too well. It was a razor-sharp line that she walked, humiliating Garak and all of Black Pine, but she did it with a brazen confidence that he couldn't help but respect.

"As for our dispute, I will let each orc make her own decision. Those who wish to join your clan and bear you orclings are free to leave and have my blessing to do so. But those who choose the warrior's path will follow me into the wilderness, and none of you shall oppose us!"

"My warriors will not suffer this humiliation," said Garak in the bitter silence that followed Nari's words. She glanced down at him and scowled.

"They will if you order them to. Or shall I kill you and let your warriors fight amongst themselves to see who shall be your successor?"

"You make it very hard for me, Nari. If you send me back to my clan in shame, it will be difficult to lead them."

"That is not my concern. Will you order your warriors to stand down, or shall I dispatch you now?"

Garak growled, his anger rising, but he had little choice. If his warriors took up arms to avenge him, many would die needlessly. The shame of defeat was a terrible burden, but for the good of the clan, he would have to bear it.

"Very well, Nari-Sen. Let me address my warriors."

She nodded and stepped back. His wounds burned and his old muscles ached, but he swallowed the pain and stood.

"It has been decided," he said in a loud voice. "Nari-Sen has won the right, and her judgment is fair. Let those who will follow her pass, and let those who will join us do so!"

He picked up Blacknife and returned it to his scabbard. Before returning to his warriors, he turned to face his victorious opponent. She stood tall and un-cowed, as cognizant of her achievement as any orcish war chief. Indeed, with the early morning sunlight gleaming across her skin and the crisp mountain breeze tossing her thick, black hair, she had the ap-pearance of a legend.

"You play a dangerous game," Garak told her. "But the orcs of Black Pine thank you."

"As do I, Garak-Nur."

He saw then that by taking the extra she-orcs, he was relieving her of a tremendous burden. And with that burden lifted, she was free to lead her fearless she-warriors on to glory.

At least my defeat was not in vain, Garak thought as they nodded and parted ways. *For Nari-Sen or for Black Pine.* Already, the she-orcs had begun to cross over, running across the hill with glee. More than half of Nari's war party seemed ready and eager to join them—enough to fully replenish the clan.

But how long they would let him lead them—that remained to be seen.

The new she-orcs were all too willing to join with Black Pine. They had sided with Nari-Sen to escape the breeding demands of the Witch-King, but few of them shared her vision of sexless freedom. All they really wanted was to return to the old ways, when the warriors fought for their own clans and not for some far-off sorcerer.

In the days that followed, many of the younger warriors began to take harems of their own. Among these was Ilika-Zan, who took only two concubines. The first was a defector from Nari-Sen, an enormous she-orc who had already borne several orclings and would no doubt bear several more. The other was Enid.

Garak wondered at Ilika's decision to take his estranged former concubine, but he had little opportunity to discuss it. As he had predicted, his humiliation at the hands of Nari-Sen had diminished his ability to lead, and those with ambition seized upon it.

Two of his warriors challenged him directly, and he made quick work of them, slaying them in combat as the rest of the clan watched on. The second wounded him in the side before Blacknife dispatched him, but somehow Garak managed to hide it. That was fortunate, since every would-be challenger would immediately rise up against him had he shown any sign of weakness.

The respite was brief, however. Those who would not dare to challenge him directly instead resorted to undermining his authority in more subtle ways. Soon, Garak had to spend nearly all of his energy maintaining his position and strengthening his own alliances within the clan. If he were younger, perhaps he could have managed it, but at his advanced age the exhaustion was too much for him, both mentally and physically. His wrinkles grew, and his hair became streaked with white.

This only served to embolden the younger warriors. A third challenger arose, and it took all of Garak's skill just to keep the young orc from slaying him. As chance would have it, his opponent slipped on a loose floor tile, stumbling just long enough for Garak to strike the killing blow. Without that twist of fate, however, Garak would surely have been slain.

Before, Ilika-Zan had been Garak's most trusted warrior. But now when Garak confided in him, Ilika was strangely silent, giving no assistance and offering no advice. Soon, Ilika began evading him entirely, finding some way to excuse himself whenever Garak called on him for counsel. His eyes turned dark whenever Garak him, and his mood became as somber as the grave. Soon, Garak stopped calling on Ilika entirely.

But the threats to his position could not be ignored. And so, in the middle of winter, Garak organized a war party. It was folly to undertake a raid while the snows were waist deep and storms pelted the mountainside, but it was the only way for him to re-establish his authority and shed the humiliation of his defeat.

The first day's march went well enough. The sun shone low in the winter sky, and a thick coating of ice covered the top of the snowbanks, speeding their progress. By nightfall, they made it to the foothills, where the snows were not so deep and the way not so treacherous. But then, a massive storm hit, all but burying them. Four warriors died of exposure, with many others suffering severe frostbite. In the face of nature's fury, it was all they could do to stay alive.

"This is madness!" Ilika roared on the fifth day. "There is no glory in battling the elements! Why are we here, when we could be safe in our burrows?"

"That's enough," Garak snapped. "I'll suffer no more insubordination. The next orc who speaks against me had better be ready to raise his sword."

"The next orc?" said Ilika, rising from his seat beside the fire. "If that is a call for a challenge, Garak, I accept. Assemble the warriors, and choose the site of our duel."

Garak was stunned beyond words. After all he and Ilika had been through together, he had almost come to believe that this day would never come. But shock soon gave way to anger, and anger to bloodlust.

"So my most loyal warrior now covets my position as war chief! Well then, Ilika, draw your sword and meet me at the top of the hill behind our camp. It has been too long since Blacknife has been greased with blood."

Ilika said nothing, though his eyes burned with rage. He drew his sword and stormed off to the hill, a dozen warriors following.

The storm had abated, and the landscape was coated in the purest white. As Garak sharpened his sword in preparation for the coming duel, an awful sadness came over him. *Ilika,* he thought to himself, *my loyal Ilika-Zan. Has Enid's tongue poisoned you against me? Is that why you seek to destroy me?* He stared up at the clear blue sky, and the mountain in which his orcs had made their home. They were an established clan now—the first few orclings had been born, with many more coming soon on the way. Food stores were low, but there was plenty of game in the wilderness to sustain them until spring. The next generation of orclings was about to be born, and Nili had made great progress in transforming the dwarvish ruins into a proper burrows. He suddenly desired to see her again, and not only her, but Bira. Since their exodus from Great Crag, Bira had truly blossomed, becoming a second mother to the clan. His wound ached, and he realized with clarity born of long experience that the duel with Ilika would almost certainly be his last. Still, it was too late to turn back now.

Whatever fate held for him, he would draw his sword and face it head-on.

When he reached the top of the hill, he saw that the whole war party had already assembled. Ilika-Zan stood at the center of the circle, the snow packed down in a wide area all around him. His sword was drawn, and his face was as impassive as stone.

"So!" Garak snarled. "The whiteness of the snow is too bright for your tastes? Let us turn it black, then—black with your blood!"

Ilika raised his sword. "You have led the clan well, Garak-Nur, and I do not have the heart to taunt you. But your defeat to Nari-Sen has addled your mind, and your pride has turned to folly. You are no longer fit to be war chief!"

"And you think you can lead the clan better?" Even as the words escaped Garak's mouth, he knew that there was no better warrior to take his place than Ilika.

"The time for words has passed, Garak. Raise your sword!"

Garak lifted Blacknife high over his head and charged with a blood-curdling scream. Ilika blocked high and stepped into the attack, but Garak elbowed him in the face and sent him stumbling backwards. He recovered quickly, though, deflecting Garak's assault.

For several minutes, the two battle-hardened veterans swung at each other. Though Garak was clearly stronger, he lacked the agility and vigor of his skillful opponent. The two were clearly matched, and neither had the upper hand.

I cannot bring myself to kill him, Garak realized as their blades clashed in the wintry air. *The clan still needs, him and we have both been friends for too long.* He deflected Ilika's blows, but his heart was not in his own.

As he leaped aside to avoid Ilika's blade, the wound in his side tore open. He gasped in pain and staggered back, lifting Blacknife weakly to deflect the next blow. Ilika saw his opportunity and swung his blade upward in a reaping arc. The swords clashed one last time in the wintry air, and Blacknife flew from his hands.

With a furious battle cry, Ilika plunged his sword into Garak's belly. Pain exploded like dragon's fire, and blood gushed from the wound like brackish water. He fell backward into the snow, the edges of his vision blurring rapidly as his breath became short and ragged.

"I'm sorry," Ilika whispered as he knelt over him. "Gods below, Garak—I'm sorry it came to this."

"It was... Enid... wasn't it?"

Ilika bit his lip and nodded.

"No matter," Garak said. He coughed, and a trickle of blood ran down the edges of his lips. "It is... better this way. You will make... a fine war chief... and this hill... is a good place... to die."

He closed his eyes, and his age-worn spirit rose from the blackened snow to enter the formless void.

The Open Source Time Machine

"Ah, Mr. Thompson, sir, so good to see you—and the other members of the board as well. How are you? I hope I'm not too late. You know how it is, always running out of time."

Carl Kearsley could not have been more out of place among the dark suits and leather briefcases. He wore grease-stained jeans and a dirty lab-coat, clothes better suited for his messy workshop than a corporate board meeting. Even so, he shook every hand as vigorously as he could, hoping to convey a sense of confidence that inwardly he lacked.

Mr. Thompson grunted as he sat down at the head of the conference table. "Very well, Mr. Kearsley. Let's get started."

"Of course, of course," said Carl, nearly tripping over his ungainly feet. Only when he looked down the long mahogany table at the long rows of black leather chairs and the balding, heavyset men occupying them did the sinking weight of fear begin to weigh on him. He hesitated for the briefest of moments before masking it with a smile and returning to his natural state of enthusiasm.

"Gentlemen, I am so glad that you could make the time to meet with me. As I'm sure you already—"

"Let's cut to the chase," said Mr. Thompson. He sat on the far end of the table, facing Carl directly with his unflinching gaze. "We've sunk almost fifty thousand dollars into your project, with precious little to show for it. Now, you've had a lot of good ideas before—none of us is claiming that you haven't—but what you're asking is, quite frankly, audacious. We're giving you one last chance to make your case before we pull out. Just why do you think this project of yours isn't a gaping money hole?"

"Why?" said Carl, his knees quivering ever so slightly. "I'll tell you why, gentlemen. Ever since the dawn of civilization, humanity has been a slave to the inexorable, relentless, unforgiving beat of the clock. Time, as we experience it, flows only in one direction, but—"

"We've all heard the sales pitch, Mr. Kearsley," said one of the men. "What we want is results. Why should we believe that you can build a functional time machine?"

"Why, haven't you read my father's notes?" Carl asked, his hands turning clammy. "The math—he proved that time is multi-dimensional. And I've continued his work, demonstrating that the intersection between temporal continua is—"

"Your father's work is practically undecipherable," said the only woman seated at the table. "Our R&D team can't make any sense of it, and our consultants tell us that there are flaws with the math." With her stern features and icy glare, she reminded Carl of his second grade teacher—the one who had made school a living hell the year after his father had gone missing.

Carl Kearsley clenched his fists, taking a deep breath. "My father's math is sound," he answered, his voice low. "He was a brilliant man, and I'm going to prove it."

"While your enthusiasm is admirable, Mr. Kearsley, you still haven't shown us why we should continue to sink funding into your project."

"But what about the time-skip experiment? Surely you can't deny that was a success."

"Your machine broke down almost as soon as you turned it on, and the results were dubious and underwhelming. Unless you can replicate—"

"But I can—I can! All I need is some money for the repairs."

Mr. Thompson sighed. "I'm afraid we can't do that, Mr. Kearsley. We have a responsibility to our shareholders, and this project shows no sign of ever becoming profitable."

Carl took a deep breath and looked from face to face. None of them showed an ounce of sympathy. He thought of his father, laboring for years against the same contempt and derision. There was only one way left to save the project, but it required a leap of faith that was absolutely terrifying. If it succeeded, it would vindicate his father beyond any doubt, but if it failed...

"Very well," he said, his hands shaking. "You asked to see results, gentlemen. Well, prepare yourselves."

As he strode to the door, he felt as if he were standing on the pinnacle of one of the most important moments of his life—a crossroads that would decide the entire course of his future.

"Time is multi-dimensional. This necessarily alters our conventional understanding of cause and effect. Until now, we have only been able to consult the past in order to look to the future. But assuming time travel is possible, why not consult the future itself?"

"What are you talking about?" asked the woman with the icy glare.

"Simply this," said Carl, turning to face them with his hand on the door knob. "With a functional time machine, I could travel to any moment in history and interact with it. I could even come back to this very meeting. So much hangs in the balance right now. You've made it clear that without results, my funding will be discontinued. Well, gentlemen, witness my results!"

He flung open the door, hoping desperately to come face to face with a future version of himself. The door swung on its hinges until it banged against the wall of the conference room, cracking the drywall and leaving a sizable dent. The executives and investors leaned forward, but the hallway was empty—no one was there.

"Is there something you want us to see, Doctor?"

Carl's stomach sank, and his legs turned to water. He opened his mouth, but could not speak. His greatest fear had been realized.

"I'm afraid we can no longer continue to fund your project, Doctor Kearsley," said Mr. Thompson as he closed the cover on his tablet. "This meeting is adjourned."

The awful, sinking weight of despair gnawed on Carl Kearsley all through the long ride back to his home. The bumper to bumper traffic only made it worse. Sitting alone in his car, locked in the hazy gridlock, there was nothing to distract him from the truth that all his life's work had been in vain.

Why had his future self failed to appear? What flaw in the causal matrix had prevented him from coming back? Time was not linear—his father had proven as much. According to the multidimensional nature of the matrix, it made perfect sense for his future self to use the finished time machine in order to secure the funding. Such loops of causality were not forbidden—in fact, the math encouraged them. So where was the flaw?

The only explanation was the one that he'd feared from the moment he'd taken up his father's work: that time travel was fundamentally impossible. That was the shadow of fear under which Carl had labored all his life, and now, the shadow had become a reality. If he could not travel back in time to save his own project, then perhaps he would never build the time machine at all.

As he sat in traffic, inching along at a pace that made eternity seem like more than an abstract concept, his thoughts wandered to his father, laboring in obscurity for so many years before his abrupt and unexplained disappearance. All his life, he had faced cynicism and doubt, but had continued his work even in the face of setbacks and discouragement. He had never seen his dream come to fruition, but had pursued it relentlessly nonetheless. Carl wished that he had known the man not just as a father figure, but as a fellow inventor. He had dedicated his life to vindicating his father's work, but now it seemed that all of his efforts had been in vain.

He reached his house long after sunset. The last hues of the rapidly fading twilight had all but disappeared, and the lights of the city drowned out all but the brightest stars. With a heavy heart, he walked past his unkempt, weed-filled lawn and up the creaky steps to his front porch.

To his surprise, the lights were on inside.

He frowned. Had he left them on when he'd left in the morning? Though possible, it was highly unlikely. He'd installed a timer on the kitchen light switch to prevent that very thing, and while it was hard to tell from the front porch window, the kitchen light seemed to be the one that was on.

With healthy dose of caution, he unlocked the door and stepped quietly inside. Sure enough, it was the kitchen light. The smell of freshly ground coffee met his nose, making him frown. Someone was in his house—someone who didn't belong there.

"Hello?" he called out, his heart racing. "Who's there?"

"Only you," came a voice, followed by a loud chuckle. "In a manner of speaking, of course."

Carl rounded the corner and came face to face with the strangest, most disorienting sight of his life. Sitting at his kitchen table was a man who resembled himself in every way, down to the lab coat and dirty jeans. He was drinking coffee from his favorite mug—the one that said "this might be vodka" on the side. He grinned as if it was his house, not Carl's.

"Who are you?" Carl asked, his cheeks turning pale.

"I told you, Carl," said the man. "I'm you."

Realization struck him like a bolt of lightning. "You—you're me? From the future?"

"Precisely."

Like the earth-shattering crack of thunder follow-ing lightning at a slight delay, Carl's realization quickly turned to rage. "What are you doing here?" he shouted. "Why didn't you come at the board meet-ing, when I expected you? Do you realize what you've done?"

"Of course I do. The board has cut your funding and dropped your project."

"Then why didn't you stop that?"

"Because that's the best thing that's happened to you," said his future self. He gestured to the chair next to him. "Care to have a seat?"

"What? No!" screamed Carl. "Do you—what do you mean, losing my funding was the best thing to happen to me?"

"Why do you think?"

The question did more to calm him than anything else could. As his mind set to work on the answer, his rage slowly deflated. He sat down in the offered chair.

"I—I don't know. I needed the money to repair my equipment after the failed time-skip experiment. Without it, I don't know if I'll ever be able to complete the research that I need in order to build a functioning machine."

"And yet here I am, speaking with you. Therefore, you obviously found a way to do it."

"But why put it on me to develop this technology by myself? Wouldn't it be easier to get the financial backing of a large corporation—wasn't that the plan from the beginning?"

His future self smiled. "Now you're asking the right questions. And since you're listening, I'll give you the answers, after asking a few questions of my own. First, what makes you think that corporate funding is your only option?"

The question took Carl back. "I—I don't know. I just assumed that that was the only way to get the capital that I needed."

"But isn't time multi-dimensional? What made you believe that the only resources available to you were the ones in the present?"

"Because—well, because at the time that's all I had," Carl stammered. It was a lame answer, and he knew it. His future self evidently knew this, because he merely raised an eyebrow without belaboring the point.

"Second question: what makes you think that it's easier to go the corporate route? To sell out your copyright and lock down the technology with patents?"

"Well, it's the best way I could see to raise the capital," Carl said. Like a spectator at a debate, or a long-time lurker on a spirited message board, he could see where his future self was going with this.

"The fastest way, perhaps, but what about the long-term effects of such a choice? Do you know what would happen if the technology became proprietary?"

"I suppose it would lead to a great deal of problems."

"That's putting it lightly," said his future self. "Time is not linear—it's multi-dimensional, just like father proved. That means that for any given moment, there are countless alternative timelines that exist apart from the one we are experiencing. I've only explored a few of them, but I've seen enough to know that it's easy to screw things up. And what in this universe is better at screwing things up than a bloated corporate bureaucracy?"

"So you're saying that if I did get the corporate funding, it would lead to disaster?"

"Precisely. If you want to serve the time traveling community, the best thing you can do is to keep the technology free."

Carl blinked. "The time traveling community?"

"Of course! Did you honestly think you were the only one?"

"Well, no, but—you mean there are time travelers among us?"

His question elicited a deep belly laugh from his future self. "If only you could see your face right now! You will, of course, but that's not the point. Yes, there's a community of time travelers. We're a lot more prevalent than you might think. Benjamin Franklin, Martin Luther, Satoshi Nakamoto—you'd be surprised to learn just how many of us there are. Though not all of us see eye to eye. Hitler, for example—"

"Hitler was a time traveler?"

The future version of himself sighed. "Yes, I'm afraid. That's why none of us have been able to eliminate him from the matrix entirely. By the way, when does Hitler die in this timeline?"

"Uh, 1945."

"In a bunker? At the end of the war?"

"Yes."

"Ah, so we did manage to stop him! Good—very good."

"Wait," said Carl. "You're telling me that all of history has been shaped by time travelers?"

"Precisely. That's why it's so important to keep the technology open source. There are a number of timelines in which the technology becomes proprietary, and all of them collapse into paradox and chaos. Time just wants to be free."

"But—but how did you develop the technology in the first place? How am I supposed to develop it?"

His future self grinned. "Good question," he said, fishing into the front right pocket of his lab coat. "You'll develop it the same way I did: through collaboration."

He reached out and handed Carl a flash drive. The casing was black and made of plastic, with an empty keyring and a retractable USB head. It looked like one of the many flash drives in the upper drawer of his workshop computer desk. Chills shot down Carl's back as he took it—perhaps the present-day version of the same drive was lying in his desk right now.

"I must go, but I wish you the best of luck. A great work lies before you, one in which you will not be alone. Farewell, and remember: time wants to be free!"

The air around Carl's future self began to shimmer, and the light seemed to gather immediately around his person. It became brighter and brighter until Carl had to shield his eyes—and then, in a flash, his future self disappeared into thin air. His coffee mug sat on the table where his future self had left it, half empty and still steaming. The lights were on, the chair was pulled back, but most importantly, the flash drive was still clenched in his sweaty hand.

Carl wasted no time. As quickly as he could, he sprinted to his workshop and turned on his computer, tapping impatiently as it booted up. The moment it was ready, he plugged in the flash drive from the future and brought up its contents. It contained a list of blueprint files and text documents with names like "FUNDAMENTALS," "APPLICATIONS," and "METHODS." On a whim, he opened the file named "FUNDAMENTALS" and began to skim over it. As he did, his heart began to race and an insuppressible grin spread across his face.

This was it—this was what he'd spent his whole life working on! Every problem he'd toiled unsuccessfully over, every paradox he'd spent sleepless nights trying to unravel—the solutions were all plain before him. Some of them were clearer than others—there would still be something of a learning curve trying to put it all together—but still, given enough time, he had full confidence he'd be able to do it.

He worked through the night and into the early morning. By the time he finally left his workshop to collapse exhausted on his bed, his mind was swimming with the possibilities. This was the dream his father had spent his life working toward. If only he had lived to see it—but then again, why not? Time wasn't linear, it was multi-dimensional, allowing for all manner of loops and interwoven causalities. And when his home-built time machine was fully functional, thanks to the open source ethic of the time travel community, then perhaps Carl would be able to go back and meet his father. Perhaps one day, they would even be able to collaborate.

Author's Note

This collection has been a long time in coming. I wrote the oldest story ("Decision LZ1527") while still in college, and the latest story ("Jane Carter of Earth and the Rescue that Never Was") about eight years after I graduated and two years before I got married. During that time, I took my writing from a hobby to a profession, switched from pursuing a traditional career to writing indie, and final started to get my feet under me as an indie writer.

I have yet to meet someone who makes a living writing short stories. Eric James Stone is a close friend of our family (his wife was Mrs. Vasicek's college roommate, and they live in our neighborhood here in Utah), and he's probably the most successful short story writer I know. Even he concedes that it's not worth writing for the money. I still think it's theoretically possible, if you average 2 new stories a week (100 per year), sell at least half of them to professional-paying markets, and live in a van down by the river.

So why do I write short stories? Most of the time, it's because I have a really interesting idea that's compelling enough to demand its own story, but not big enough to fill a whole novel. That's why so many of my shorts tend to be time travel stories.

Sometimes, an idea sticks in my head for a very long time before it demands to be written. "The Curse of the Lifewalker" grew out of an experience in Boy Scout summer camp when I found a young sapling growing out of the stump of an American Chestnut, and the scout leaders told me about the blight that killed them all off. Other times, I write a story almost as soon as the idea comes to me. I saw "is this the hill on which you want to die?" in the comments section of an online news article, and it immediately became the inspiration for "A Hill On Which To Die," which I finished a few weeks later. I wrote "The Open Source Time Machine" after making the switch to Linux, and "The Gettysburg Paradox" after reading Michael and Jeff Shaara's Civil War Trilogy.

Sometimes, the ideas are so compelling that I can hardly do anything else until they're written. For "Memoirs of a Snowflake," I was visiting a friend in college to write in his basement during a heavy snowstorm. While crossing the street to get there, the idea suddenly struck me and I couldn't write anything else. "Killing Mister Wilson" was similar, but the reasons were more political in nature (2016 was a strange year). Other ideas aren't quite as demanding, but in the process of writing them, you infuse it with some essential part of yourself that makes it compelling on its own. "Time and Space in Amish Country" was like that: I graduated in the middle of the Great Recession and it took me years to get on my feet. I wasn't expecting for that personal experience to come out, but it did, and the story practically wrote itself.

Some stories are written with a clear audience and purpose in mind. I wrote "Jane Carter of Earth and the Rescue that Never Was" as a tie-in to my Gunslinger Trilogy books: *Gunslinger to the Stars, Gunslinger to the Galaxy,* and *Gunslinger to Earth.* The goal was to give my readers a story to introduce them to the characters and the world, but it worked pretty well on its own too. Others go in a completely different direction from what I intended. "My Name Is For My Friends" started as the prologue for a novel, but when I realized that it made a decent story on its own I decided to take it that route. I never finished the novel.

One of the nice things about short stories is that it's something you can finish relatively quickly and say "look! I accomplished something!" When I'm struggling through the messy middle of a novel, I'll sometimes take a quick break to write a short story. Besides the ego boost, it's also something that I can offer my readers in the off-months between novel releases.

I generally try to sell my short stories to traditional markets, like magazines or anthologies, before I self-publish them. In doing so, I've been privileged to meet and work with a lot of really great people. Most of the stories in this volume have found a home in some traditional market. It can be a bit tricky, though, because most markets want original stories (not reprints), and most prefer that you don't send them simultaneous submissions (stories that are submitted to multiple places at once). It is possible to keep a story on submission for years, only for it to never find a home—at least, not one that pays well enough to make it worthwhile. In the meantime, that's a story you could have indie-published and gotten out to your readers that much sooner. But indie-published short story singles generally earn so little that you'll make a whole lot more with a pro or even a semi-pro sale... but at what point is it worth it to just cut your losses and publish it yourself?

Right now (April 2020), my personal rule is to limit each story to between 25 and 30 submissions before self-publishing it. That's about two hours worth of work, and at the rate at which I value my time, it doesn't make sense to keep pushing for a traditional publication. After thirty submissions, I've usually exhausted all of the professional paying markets anyway. I do keep my stories on submission to the reprint markets after I've published them indie, but the lowest rate I'm willing to accept is 1 cent per word. I used to go with the token paying markets, but I've found that it just isn't worth it.

I haven't had a whole lot of success with my indie-published singles, but they do earn a small trickle of royalties. What they're really useful for is giveaways and newsletter builders. I'm sure that many of you reading this author's note first heard of me when you picked up one of my short stories on Book Funnel or

Story Origin. The trouble with trying to sell them is that they can only really command about $0.99 on the market, but at that price point the royalty rates are typically only 35%. Dean Wesley Smith claims that you can price short stories at $2.99, but that seems like too much to me. The other thing about publishing single short stories is that after a while, they come to dominate your catalog. I'd much rather have my novels serve as a reader's first impression of me. At the same time, though, I do want my short stories to be available for the readers who are looking for them. I've tried publishing them in bundles of 3 or 5 the way Dean recommends, but those sold even fewer copies than my singles.

The conclusion I've drawn from all of this is that short story readers prefer collections over single short stories, and large collections over small ones. Which makes sense. There are so many options for free stories now: podcasts like Drabblecast or Escape Pod, or free online magazines like Clarkesworld and Strange Horizons. There are even some publications like The Arcanist or Daily Science Fiction that deliver stories direct to your email. With so many free options for truly great and high quality short fiction, the only real reason to buy a collection is so that you can get a whole bunch of them in one place from one author (or selected by one editor).

In putting this collection together, I decided to assemble as many stories as it would take to get it over 40,000 words, which is the length at which SFWA (Science Fiction & Fantasy Writers of America) defines a book as a novel. I hope you feel that's enough stories to provide a good value. I was originally going to do a themed collection, but one of my writer friends who does a lot of short stories told me that most of her readers actually prefer a healthy variety. If you're one of those readers who prefer that all the stories keep to the same genre or theme, my next collection will be nothing but space opera; I'm just waiting for some of the rights to revert back to me. As with this one, that collection will have at least 40k words of fiction.

If you enjoyed this short story collection, I would be honored if you took the time to post an honest review. It not only helps and encourages me; it also helps other readers find great books. If you want to follow me, the best way to do that is to subscribe to my email newsletter, which I send out about 3-4 times per month. I don't really do social media at this point, partly out of privacy concerns, partly as a quality of life issue. However, if you want to see what I'm reading, you can follow me on Goodreads.

That just about does it for this one. I say this in every author's note, but I genuinely mean it: thank you for reading!

Joe
June 2020
HTTL

Acknowledgments

First, I owe a huge thanks to David Steffen and all the folks behind The Submission Grinder, which is what I use to manage all of my short story submissions. I can't imagine how much work they've put into the site, and it has proven absolutely invaluable for my career. Thank you so much for all that you do.

For "The Gettysburg Paradox," thanks to Kevin Frost of Gallery of Curiosities for his editorial feedback. For "Killing Mister Wilson," thanks to Scott Slack and Scott "Toad" Bascom for their help in spitballing the story idea. For "My Name Is For My Friends," thanks to my favorite fantasy author, the late David Gemmell, for the books of his that changed my life and inspired me to write this story. For "Memoirs of a Snowflake," thanks to my old college writing group, especially Evan Witt, Nicholas Rose, Annaliese Lemmon, Ben Hardin, Kindal and Emily Debenham, and Aneeka Richins.

For "The Curse of the Lifewalker," thanks again to Nicholas Rose and Scott "Toad" Bascom, as well as

Mykle Law for their help with the story. For "Decision LZ1527," thanks to my old college writing group again, as well as my college roommate Steve Dethloff and the 2009 staff of *Leading Edge Magazine,* especially Camilla Parshall, Kristy Gilbert, and Chris Baxter. For "Jane Carter and the Rescue that Never Was," thanks again to Scott "Toad" Bascom and also for his extensive help with *Gunslinger to the Stars,* which was invaluable.

For "Time and Space in Amish Country," thanks to my Mom for all those Amtrak tickets over the years. Sixty-plus hours from Salt Lake City to Springfield Massachusetts was excrutiating at times (especially the summer my girlfriend broke up with me four hours out of Chicago), but it did make the story possible. For "A Hill On Which To Die," thanks to my old roommates Ben Keeley and Jeff Jensen for their helpful feedback, and for Scott "Toad" Bascom and the Kearsleys for helping to workshop it. And lastly, for "The Open Source Time Machine," thanks to Mykle Law for helping install Ubuntu on my netbook and getting me into Linux.

Thanks everyone! Without your help, these stories would not have turned out the way they did!